Courting
Miss Lancaster

Courting
MISS LANCASTER
a novel

Sarah M. Eden

Covenant Communications, Inc.

Cover photography by McKenzie Deakins, photographybymckenzie.com. Cover image: *Colorful Cottage Gardens* © fotoVoyager, courtesy iStockphoto. Author photo © Claire Waite.

Cover design © 2010 by Covenant Communications, Inc.

Published by Covenant Communications, Inc.
American Fork, Utah

Printed in The United States of America
First Printing: March 2010

16 15 14 13 12 11 10   10 9 8 7 6 5 4 3 2 1

ISBN-13: 978-1-60861-000-6

To Annette, who knows talent when she sees it and, in a moment of delirium, lumped me into that group.

Chapter 1

"FIRST THING IN THE MORNING, I am throwing her in the Thames."

Harry Windover grinned, though he was certain the dire pronouncement from the Duke of Kielder was meant to inspire anxious concern. While the rest of England trembled at the slightest hint of a threat from the infamous duke, Harry's friendship with the notorious nobleman was of long-enough standing to allow him greater insight into the gentleman's character. Adam Boyce, Duke of Kielder, was more than capable of and, if truth be told, entirely willing to follow through with the most drastic of threats. But, though he growled regularly, he acted rationally.

"And what has this doomed female done to deserve such an unenviable fate?" Harry asked, smiling still.

"She requires a Season," Adam declared, his tone clearly communicating his utter disapproval as well as his complete disbelief.

"Most young ladies do," Harry answered. "How else are the poor dears' parents to see them married to the highest bidder, er, most suitable gentleman?"

He almost laughed at the black look Adam gave him. Adam had redefined "highest bidder" in his courtship. If one were being picky, *courtship* would not be the word to describe Adam's successful acquiring of a bride. He'd written a letter, offered the equivalent of several small fortunes, and had been married—all within a few short weeks. Those gentlemen, like Harry, who did not possess one small fortune, let alone several entirely disposable ones, found themselves perpetually unsought-after, ineligible, and very, very single.

"Dare I ask why this particular young lady's very commonplace requirement has warranted the ending of her no-doubt short life?"

"If she is dead, she will not need a Season."

"True, but she would need a wake and a funeral. Those, too, can be tedious."

"But far shorter in duration."

A young gentleman, probably having no more than twenty years in his dish, passed near the chairs in the back of White's, where Harry and Adam were spending the afternoon. With one look, Adam sent the young cub scurrying in the opposite direction, a look of pale-faced fear crossing his features.

Harry chuckled. "Must you torture the infantry?"

Adam ignored him. Which made Harry laugh more. It was their pattern, had been since their days at Harrow. Adam put on his "Fearsome Duke" façade. Harry laughed at the absurdity of it—he knowing that Adam was a good-hearted person beneath it—and that made Adam grumpy. Adam, Harry knew very well, realized he was a different person beneath his ironclad mask, and it unsettled him to think that his armor could be pierced. Adam hadn't yet tossed Harry over, nor run him through, though he had many times threatened to do so.

Harry returned to the subject at hand. "Countless young ladies have their Seasons each year, Adam. Why should this particular case upset you so entirely?"

"In this particular case, I have the dubious distinction of being the debutante's guardian."

For a fraction of a second, Harry's breath caught. He was certain he knew the identity of the soon-to-be victim of Adam's distemper. *Athena Lancaster.* "You did apply for legal guardianship of your wife's sisters and brother," Harry reminded him. "When one acquires sisters-in-law, and when one has provided them with the kingdom's most enviable dowries, such things as Seasons must be assumed."

"I assumed guardianship because their father is losing hold of his faculties," Adam corrected. "But if I am forced through the tedium of a come-out, I shall lose hold of mine."

"And then where shall we be?" Harry laughed.

"My sanity is a source of amusement to you?" Adam raised that universally feared eyebrow.

"Everything about you is a source of amusement to me." Harry smiled.

"I should call you out for that," Adam threatened.

"As much fun as that would be, it does not solve *your* problem."

Adam harrumphed and contented himself for a while with glaring at the other members of the club daring, or foolish, enough to sit within visual range. Harry's mind spun as Adam brooded in silence.

Athena Lancaster.

He could picture her with perfect clarity: golden curls, sparkling green eyes, creamy complexion. Athena was taller than her sister, the Duchess of Kielder, coming to Harry's chin, something he knew by virtue of having stood beside her as they'd signed as witnesses to Adam and Persephone's wedding. He'd discovered in that same moment that she smelled like violets. His sister, Jane, wore the same scent but not at all in the same way. Harry had become a favorite of the little flower girl on the corner of Piccadilly. She always carried violets. And he always bought a posy. In other words, Harry knew himself to be well and truly besotted.

It was, in all reality, a tragedy.

Athena, thanks to the desperation of her then-future brother-in-law, was exceptionally well-dowered, having £20,000. She was also the most beautiful woman of his acquaintance, an assessment he was certain would be shared by every gentleman who met her. In addition, she had the world's most overprotective guardian. Adam griped and grumbled over the inconvenience of his newly acquired wards, but Harry knew Adam secretly cared a great deal for them, due in large part to how deeply he loved their sister, his wife. And while the fearsome duke might allow Harry's friendship, there was little hope that he would look favorably on a suit for the hand of his sister-in-law from a gentleman who could boast only a marginally productive estate in the wilds of Northumberland and less than £700 per anum. Athena could do far better. Adam would make certain she did.

Harry had accepted the entire situation nearly a year earlier, within minutes of setting eyes on Athena. He had simply expected to have more time to resign himself to the fact that she would be courted by throngs of admirers with deeper pockets than his to recommend them.

"Athena arrived in London this morning with her horde of sisters in tow, along with their governess," Adam grumbled.

Athena was in London? Harry couldn't be sure if that was welcome news or not.

"The infuriating female informed me within moments of her arrival at Falstone House that she wishes to be brought out during the Little Season," Adam continued. If Harry hadn't known Adam so well, he might have taken exception to the "infuriating female" comment. "She explained that she was certain it would be a more agreeable option to *me*." His look of patent disbelief clearly displayed his evaluation of that bit of logic.

"Either Miss Lancaster"—Harry didn't feel it was safe to call the object of his regard by her Christian name in Adam's hearing—"does not realize that you flee London quite religiously every August or she feels the smaller social throng of the Little Season would be more to your liking."

"She was obviously misinformed," Adam observed.

"And did you address the subject of her misapprehension?" Harry asked, careful to keep his tone casual so Adam wouldn't guess at the slight increase in tension Harry was experiencing worrying over the outcome of Athena's encounter with Adam's testy temper.

Adam's snort put Harry at ease. Adam very seldom made noises when cutting words would suffice. "The Lancaster women are manipulative," Adam grumbled. "Athena informed me of her decision, smiled, and flitted from the room before I had a chance to say a single word. And the very next moment, Persephone was in my book room thanking me rather . . . gushingly for taking such wonderful care of her sisters. By the time I realized I was being distracted, the arrangements were already being undertaken."

Harry chuckled. "Manipulative, indeed." And very well planned. He knew Persephone had a good head on her shoulders, and he suspected Athena did as well. One could not, after all, be named for the Greek goddess of divine intelligence and be a complete featherhead.

"I have half a mind to return to Falstone Castle and leave Athena to her own devices," Adam declared. "Let her sort through the ridiculous moonlings who will line my drawing room day after tedious day. If it were up to me, I'd send every one of them packing and send Athena to a nunnery."

"Do you think she would go?" Harry chuckled.

Adam muttered something that sounded suspiciously like "Lancaster women" and took up the paper again.

"Perhaps you should hire out, Adam," Harry laughingly suggested. "Put an advertisement in the *Times* requesting the services of . . . How would one put that, exactly? . . . of an expe-rienced suitor sorter. You would, of course, have to find someone who knew *society* and could sort the bad apples from the horrible apples and who not only could endure the endless prattle of the social whirl but, preferably, enjoy it."

"If your estate ever completely falls to ruin, Harry, you could hire yourself out for just such a position," Adam said, stiffening his paper and allowing his scowl to settle on its pages. "You have described yourself perfectly."

Harry laughed, earning a look of amazement from the youngling Adam had earlier sent into life-threatening palpita-tions of fear. Harry got that look a lot. Anyone who regularly laughed in the duke's presence was either entirely mad or placed very little value on the continuation of his existence. It was a rather fine line, when he thought about it. Rather like being a court jester in the days when royalty could behead on a whim.

The sudden jerking of Adam's paper should have been a warning. But Harry missed it, something he was later certain he would regret time and again.

"Suitor sorter," Adam quite suddenly said, a look on his usually somber face that on anyone else might have been described as gleeful. "Harry, name your price."

"My what?" Harry chuckled, certain Adam was truly addled.

"For taking over the tedious aspects of this ridiculous come-out."

"I beg your—"

"Don't be obtuse," Adam snapped at him. The gleeful look was gone. "I have no desire to spend every night of the next few months at balls and soirees or drowning in tea with morning callers. You relish such things."

"You are asking me to help your sister-in-law find a husband?" Adam couldn't possibly have known the irony of that request.

"Only to sort out the bad apples, as you said," Adam corrected. "I'll handle the formalities."

"Like tearing limb by limb any less-than-worthies who apply for her hand?"

Adam's face clearly communicated the joy he would find in that undertaking. "But the social niceties, I could do without. And as you are an almost constant guest in the house and a family acquaintance of inordinately long standing—"

Harry held up his hands in a gesture of surrender. He had only a shabby set of rooms in London to call his own and lacked the means of living in any semblance of style. He would not go to Falstone Castle in Northumberland when Adam was not there, and visiting his own dilapidated estate was always an exercise in futile frustration. One needed capital to repair generations of neglect—capital he did not have. Being the constant guest of his oldest friend was something of a necessity, a means of obtaining regular food and sitting in warmth he did not have to pay for. Adam had never asked anything of him in return for his hospitality. But Harry could not, in good conscience, deny Adam a favor when he wished for it.

"Just sort through the bushel?" Harry asked doubtfully.

"Unless you think Athena will receive little attention." Adam raised an eyebrow. He obviously knew Athena would be something of an immediate sensation when she made her bows to society.

Harry shook his head. "She will receive ample attention," he answered, trying not to grumble.

"And it is crucial that the less-than-deserving be dispatched rather immediately," Adam answered.

Something in the wording of that appealed to Harry. Dispatching the less-than-deserving. He couldn't have her for himself, he understood that. But he could see to it that she found a gentleman who would treat her well, who would care for more than her dowry and connections. It would be torture, no denying that, but there would be at least a measure of satisfaction in the undertaking.

"Perhaps you should define 'less-than-deserving,'" Harry ventured.

Adam gave Harry the look he reserved for moments when Harry didn't live up to Adam's standard of intelligence. "Philanderers, divorcés, rogues and rakes, anyone whose standing is not at least among the gentry, anyone too old or too young. Certainly no one stupid or cowardly. Absolutely no member of my extended family." Harry actually smiled at that. There were few people in Adam's extended family, and Harry knew Adam heartily disapproved of every last one of them. "And under no circumstances should she be permitted to be courted by a fortune hunter. A fortune hunter is one thing I will absolutely not abide."

And that was the death knoll to any flicker of hope Harry might have had. While he cared little for Athena's dowry, he knew himself to be pathetically short of funds. In the eyes of the world, even in the eyes of his best friend, Harry would be seen as that most despised of creatures: the dreaded fortune hunter.

"I believe I can steer Miss Lancaster clear of any undesirable types," Harry said, resigning himself to a torturous few months—*weeks* if Athena was as popular as he expected she would be.

"Then let us hope she does not descend upon you with demands and ideas." Adam shook his head with weary disbelief. "*You* will hardly be rid of her through the Little Season."

Hardly be rid of her.

A smile crept across Harry's face.

A few weeks with Athena. The few hours he'd spent with her after Adam's wedding had been more than pleasant. He'd spent time with her again over the Christmas holiday. Athena and her sisters had arrived at Falstone Castle that spring several weeks before Harry's departure for London. The sweetness of her disposition had been obvious—another trait she shared with her sister—but so had her keen mind and witty sense of humor. It had only deepened his attraction to her.

"So when do I begin my duties?" Harry asked, feeling a surge of anticipation.

"As soon as the ladies are content with her wardrobe. Heaven knows that could take time."

Harry nodded absently. The next few weeks would be the most acutely torturous of his life, and he would relish every moment.

Chapter 2

A WELL-BRED YOUNG LADY DOES not cry at a ball. Athena Lancaster knew that very basic rule. She knew every rule, basic or otherwise, that governed society. She had fastidiously practiced every country dance she'd ever heard of, mentally reviewed the movements of the minuet, though she truly disliked it. She was well-versed in the many intricacies and nuances of wielding her fan and the message each movement was meant to convey. Athena had studied the copy of Debrett's she'd found in her brother-in-law's library—having slipped into that room when she was absolutely certain His Grace was away from home—and was confident she could place every member of the aristocracy into their respective families. She had trembled through her presentation and had managed not to disgrace herself before the queen. She was gowned in the first stare of fashion, her gold ringlets coiffed flatteringly.

And Athena was moments from sobbing.

She had pictured her first ball hundreds of times as a young girl. She had imagined standing poised and confident, smiling bewitchingly at the fashionable gentlemen she would meet. Athena had danced in her dreams with confidence and grace. Never in all her imaginings had she seen herself sitting on an exceedingly uncomfortable chair watching the dances slip past without a single soul soliciting her hand.

"Such a beauty," she had heard countless people say over the years. "With her sweet nature and lovely countenance, Miss Athena will make a grand match." She had rather counted on being a success, but not in a preening or self-absorbed way. Indeed, she had often seen that forthcoming "grand match" as the answer to all her family's problems. A well-heeled gentleman who loved her enough to marry her without a penny to her name would certainly possess enough generosity to save her loved ones from the threat of poverty. She had planned on it.

Athena glanced around the glittering ballroom once more. Couples glided through the steps of a country dance. Athena knew the movements by heart. How she had practiced and reviewed! Just that morning she had spent a full hour studiously covering every dance she might possibly be called on to perform. She ought to have rehearsed being rejected; that would most certainly have proven more useful.

The attempt at wit helped keep the tears at bay for the moment.

At least, Athena told herself, she'd danced once upon first arriving. Her brother in-law, the infamous Duke of Kielder, had—no doubt at the request of his wife, Athena's older sister, Persephone—stood up with her for the length of an entire quadrille. Immediately after which he had taken up his post just behind Athena's chair. Adam, as His Grace had suggested she call him when they were at home—again, probably at the suggestion of his wife—was not overly fond of going about in society. And society, Athena was fairly certain, rather supported him in that preference. He frightened people. He terrified Athena.

Around her the music was coming to its conclusion, another dance ending. With a mighty effort, Athena kept the tears at bay as she cast her eyes about, hoping a gentleman would magically materialize and request her hand for the next set. She had been at the Debensham's ball for nearly two hours. The next set was the supper dance. Many gentlemen had approached. Athena had offered a tentative smile. And, every time, moments before reaching her side, each gentleman's expression had turned from approval to dismay, and they had simply walked past her. One had actually turned on the spot and walked back in the direction from which he had come. Athena felt heat stain her cheeks as she remembered the embarrassment of that moment.

She closed her eyes for a moment, forced a calming breath, and silently uttered yet another prayer. She would survive. No matter what else went wrong, she would survive. The Lancasters were nothing if not persevering.

"Miss Lancaster."

The sound of a gentleman's voice so near her startled Athena. She opened her eyes, afraid her sudden nervousness would be embarrassingly obvious. Her discomfort slid away in an instant.

"Hello, Mr. Windover," she said with palpable relief. Mr. Windover was unfailingly kind and could be counted on to lighten even the most difficult of situations. At that moment, he was a godsend.

"About time you got here, you worthless maggot," Adam said behind Athena. She tensed at his voice, the way she always did.

"I missed you too, Your Grace." Mr. Windover grinned up at the single most dangerous man in the room. Only Mr. Windover could have done as much.

Athena very nearly smiled for the first time in hours. Adam was less frightening when Mr. Windover was nearby.

"Make yourself useful, Harry, and dance with Athena," Adam ordered.

Athena felt her cheeks flame. How horrifyingly humiliating. If her two hours of uninterrupted sitting had not confirmed her a wallflower, having her guardian order a gentleman to stand up with her certainly solidified the label.

"Bad form, old man." Mr. Windover shook his head in a mock display of disapproval. "I had intended to ask the lady myself. But now she will be convinced I am doing so only on your orders. Bad form." Mr. Windover smiled at Athena, his blue eyes twinkling down at her. "Dare I hope your supper dance is unclaimed?"

"No," Athena managed, her heart suddenly leaping. She would not be forced to sit out the supper dance!

"*No,* I ought not to hope? Or *no,* it is not claimed?" Mr. Windover smiled more broadly.

A smile slid across Athena's face. "It is unclaimed," she clarified.

"If you stand there talking endlessly like a gossiping matron, it will remain unclaimed after the music begins," Adam said. "Get on with it, sapskull."

Harry held his gloved hand out to Athena. She slipped her hand in his and rose to walk with him to the set forming nearest her seat. For only a moment, her heart fluttered nervously. But Mr. Windover smiled across at her, and she felt herself grow more at ease. He was a comfortable sort of person—a drastic change from Adam, who had been at her side the entire evening.

The quick movements of the dance made any degree of conversation between them impossible. It was just as well. Despite her frequent practicing, Athena was concentrating on her steps, determined not to embarrass herself.

The dancers, including Mr. Windover, applauded as the orchestra emitted one last, drawn-out note before the mass exodus to the supper room. Athena laid her hand quite properly on the arm Mr. Windover offered her and walked with him out of the ballroom, a little out of breath.

"I understand from your sister that your presentation went well yesterday," Mr. Windover said after they were both seated with plates of delectable food before them.

"I did not even trip once," Athena said lightly.

"And you were so certain you would." Mr. Windover smiled back. Her nervousness had been discussed at some length at a family dinner the evening before her presentation. Mr. Windover was always present at family dinners, something Athena appreciated. Persephone may have been entirely at ease with her husband, but his often surly and always intimidating presence never failed to rid Athena of her appetite. At Falstone Castle she had not been so entirely overset by him. But the combination of her fearsome brother-in-law—his disgruntled nature more keenly accentuated in London—with the prospect of a Season, even a Little one, had proven nearly too much for her nerves.

"I wish you could have been there," Athena mused, pushing a puff pastry around her plate with her fork. "Persephone was nearly as nervous as I, and His Grace looked . . ." What was the right word?

"Annoyed?" Mr. Windover ventured.

"Precisely." Athena smiled. "How did you know that? You were not even present."

"The Fearsome Duke of Kielder generally looks annoyed when interacting with the royal family," Mr. Windover whispered, leaning closer to her as he did. The last remnants of nervousness slipped away at his nearness. Mr. Windover had that effect on her, had from the moment she'd first met him at Persephone's wedding. He was calming, peaceful. "I believe he finds them tedious."

"What amazes me is that he makes no effort to hide his feelings." Athena shook her head. She could not imagine being so unconcerned with the opinions of the very highest of society. "Does he not worry that he might offend?"

"I do not believe he cares one whit if the royal family is offended by him. They, on the other hand, appear quite concerned about offending *him*," Mr. Windover answered. "The queen, I am certain, finds our duke quite fascinating. I understand she goes to great lengths to make him welcome whenever he condescends to attend her drawing rooms."

"She spoke with him for nearly ten minutes," Athena confirmed, remembering her shock at the unexpected break with convention. "Exclusively."

"And he probably glared at her the entire time," Mr. Windover added.

"He had the temerity to check the time on his pocket watch as Her Majesty was addressing him," Athena said, knowing her eyes were wide with the memory.

Mr. Windover laughed out loud. "Lands, I wish I had been there to see that."

"And he caught out the prince watching him rather pointedly and—"

"The prince was actually foolish enough to stare at the Dangerous Duke?"

Athena nodded. "And far more foolish to have been caught doing it."

"Don't tell me he called His Royal Highness out again." Mr. Windover shook his head.

"Again?" Athena felt her heart lurch. "He has previously challenged the Prince of Wales?"

"It is of no account, really. Prinny apologized. The entire thing was smoothed over."

"Good heavens," Athena muttered. What kind of guardian did she have? He wrested apologies from the prince himself and found conversation with the queen irritatingly boring. Was it any wonder Athena was so uncomfortable with him?

"Let us discuss more pleasant topics," Mr. Windover said, smiling as always. He had a very reassuring smile. "How have you enjoyed your very first ball?"

Mortified, Athena felt tears prick at her eyes the instant his question was uttered. How had she enjoyed her first ball? Not at all.

"Tears, Miss Lancaster?" Mr. Windover's voice lowered to the quietest of whispers. "That will never do."

"I am sorry," Athena whispered in reply, trying valiantly to keep herself in check.

"If you will pretend an exorbitant degree of interest in the contents of your plate," Mr. Windover suggested, "I shall endeavor to appear entirely at my ease. Then, you see, the other guests will think nothing untoward has occurred, and you may recover your poise with no one the wiser."

Athena immediately lowered her eyes to her plate, keeping her head bowed enough to hide the sudden sheen of tears evident on her lashes. A young lady did not cry at a ball. Nor did she cry over supper at a ball. A few moments of silence passed while Athena worked to rein in her emotions.

"Has someone upset you?" Mr. Windover asked, his voice still low.

"No," Athena answered, grateful for the concern she heard in his voice.

"Are you disappointed in the ball?" he ventured. "Or perhaps simply in your partners?"

That nearly undid her. "I h-haven't had any," she whispered, hearing the break in her voice.

"You haven't had any? Any partners?"

Athena glanced up. Mr. Windover's eyes were on her, a look of empathy on his face. "Except for Adam, when we first arrived. And then you. There were a few times I thought a gentleman was going to approach, but, except for you, they all, without fail, did not. One even spun around and fled." She took a shaky breath. "I am not sure what is so wrong with me that . . . that . . ."

"Miss Lancaster." Mr. Windover smiled kindly. "Do you truly believe these gentlemen did not approach you because of something they found lacking in you?"

"What other reason could there be?"

Harry shook his head, as if amused in spite of himself. "There is a rather glaringly obvious reason."

Athena furrowed her brow, confused. She couldn't think of anything beyond some monumental failing in herself that she had not discovered yet.

"I believe your lack of partners had everything to do with the fact that the Duke of Kielder was standing at your shoulder with his hand resting rather ominously on the hilt of his dress sword. I am certain many of the gentlemen in attendance were rather afraid that the infamous duke would borrow a page from not-too-distant French history and behead the aristocracy should they disgruntle him in any way."

"He scared them off," Athena surmised.

"Precisely."

It was a far more welcome possibility than the reasoning she had previously applied to the situation. Adam had frightened away her prospective partners. There might be hope for her yet. Except, she immediately amended, Adam was her guardian. Any gentleman who wished to solicit her hand for a dance would have to be willing to approach even with him hovering nearby.

"That does not bode well, does it?" Athena sighed, setting her fork beside her plate, her appetite having fled entirely.

"Never fear. Adam is not likely to attend many more social functions. Persephone is far less intimidating."

"She has been rather absent this evening," Athena observed. She hadn't seen her sister more than a half-dozen times since their arrival, though she was certain Persephone had had no more partners than Athena herself had.

"I have seen her mingling," Mr. Windover said. "She is setting the foundation of your success, Miss Lancaster. Through her conversations this evening, you will receive invitations to all those events that are necessary for you to make a splash in society. I do not doubt she was taking advantage of Adam's presence to do so. On those evenings when he is not in attendance, she will be required to remain at your side, being your faithful chaperone."

"I don't think Persephone likes to be out without her husband," Athena said. "She is inordinately fond of him."

"Incomprehensible, isn't it?" Mr. Windover smiled. "Who would ever guess that Adam could be any lady's idea of an ideal husband?"

"He certainly is not mine," Athena admitted before the incivility of her unguarded confession caused her to clamp her mouth shut and close her eyes against the flush of embarrassment staining her cheeks.

"And what, pray tell, is your idea of an ideal husband?" Mr. Windover asked. His words sounded oddly choked, no doubt the result of his shock at her indelicate words. "What sort of gentleman are you looking to capture?"

Athena thought about his question and realized, to her surprise, she wasn't entirely sure. The imaginary knight on a white charger of her girlish dreams had only two concrete characteristics: he was inordinately wealthy and deeply in love with her. The former was no longer necessary. The latter was far too personal a wish to voice out loud. "I do not truly know," she said.

"If you do not know for whom you are looking, how do you expect to find him?"

A good question, indeed. A feeling of unease settled into her stomach. Her romantic dreams were growing more elusive by the moment. "I suppose I expected to simply *know*. To recognize when . . . when . . ."

"When your prince charming deposited himself at your feet?" Mr. Windover grinned.

He made it sound so childish. To Athena, the idea had always been very romantic, exciting, wonderful. "And why shouldn't I be able to recognize the gentleman for whom my heart is searching?"

"When, by your own admission, you don't even know what it is you are looking for?" Mr. Windover shook his head in obvious disapproval, though his smile did not slip. "Haven't you even a list of some sort? A compilation of desirable characteristics, or something of that nature?"

"Certainly not." The very idea was as unromantic as she could imagine any undertaking to be. A list! As if she were off to the grocer's or inventorying linens.

"You have no prerequisites?" Mr. Windover asked doubtfully.

"Nothing beyond the most rudimentary," Athena asserted. "That he be a gentleman, in the truest sense of the word. And that he be eligible."

"So his not being married would be a basic requirement and that he not be a costermonger."

"I believe you are teasing me, Mr. Windover." Athena managed a smile as well.

"Only a little, and I will confess you have piqued my curiosity. I should very much like to know what type of gentleman could win your affection."

Something about the tone of his words made Athena blush once more.

"I believe I shall have to endeavor to see that you are introduced to a variety of gentlemen—eligible ones, of course—and see for myself the results of such an unfocused search. Though I must say, I would have expected far more cunning from a young lady named for the goddess of strategic warfare."

"Warfare?" Athena laughed, though she knew from extensive study that ladies, in general, were expected to limit themselves to smiles when they were amused. "Do you consider the endeavor of seeking a future spouse comparable to war?"

"There are times, Miss Lancaster, when matters of the heart become nothing short of a brutal, painful battle."

Chapter 3

HE WAS A GLUTTON FOR punishment. There was no other explanation for it. Why else would Harry be bringing an eligible gentleman through the hordes of humanity attending the Hardfords' musical evening toward the spot where Athena was holding court?

Adam had not deigned to attend, just as Harry and everyone else even remotely acquainted with the infamous duke's opinions on musicales could have predicted. Owing to the absence of her armed sentinel, Athena enjoyed the rousing success she ought to have enjoyed at the previous night's ball. As if enough eligible gentlemen weren't already crowding around the object of Harry's affection, he was bringing another for her to weave her spell over.

He'd spent the previous night and most of that morning concerned. No, his feelings were far closer to worry. Athena—sweet, kind, trusting Athena—was embarking on the marriage mart without so much as a strategy. The exasperating female did not even know what she wished for in a husband. Marriage was lifelong, permanent. The wrong sort of husband would be disastrous for her. She would be discontent at best, miserable at worst.

Seeing her happily married would be hard enough. Having to watch a horrible marriage slowly devour her spirit would be sheer torture.

Sort through the bad apples, Adam had said. Steer her away from those unworthy of her. Harry had simply amended the edict. He would steer her away from those who would not make her happy. He would, as much as it would pain him to do so, help her find someone decent, at the very least.

But, heaven help him, he wasn't about to deposit a paragon at her feet. He wasn't nearly that masochistic.

Athena didn't know what she wished for in a husband. Harry would simply help her formulate a list. A list of what she *didn't* want.

He guided Mr. Howard, a slight acquaintance from one of his clubs, through the crowd toward Athena, silently chastising himself for ever agreeing to aid and abet Athena's foray into the blasted auction for brides and grooms and marriages he could never truly be a part of.

"Your Grace," Harry addressed Persephone with a very appropriate bow, something they were sure to remember in public, even if their interactions in private tended toward the informality one would expect of two people on terms not unlike siblings, "might I make known to you Mr. Howard."

Persephone inclined her head in a show of condescending agreement. Harry very nearly laughed out loud. Adam had taught his wife well; she could dampen the pretensions of even the most determined of toad-eaters.

"Mr. Howard, I present to you Her Grace, the Duchess of Kielder."

Harry actually heard Mr. Howard swallow thickly at the title connected to the kingdom's most feared personage. He acquitted himself admirably, though, bowing as was expected and uttering something that resembled an expression of honor at the introduction.

Harry pressed forward, lest the poor man lose courage and back away before Athena had a chance to become acquainted with him. There would be no point in making the introductions if Athena did not have that opportunity.

Mr. Howard was presented to Miss Lancaster, and the appropriate inane comments were exchanged. Into the awkward silence that followed, Athena attempted a conversation.

"Mr. Howard," she asked, "from which part of the kingdom do you hail?"

"Essex," Mr. Howard answered quite seriously.

"Essex, I understand, is a very beautiful county," Athena offered.

Mr. Howard simply nodded. Harry felt a smile tugging at his lips. Mr. Howard was quite the least talkative person of Harry's acquaintance. It was not a result of timidity; Harry would never take advantage of a character trait that was so inherently vulnerable. Mr. Howard simply never felt the need to say much above four words at a time. And he was quite without anything resembling a sense of humor. His every remark was made somberly, whether or not such a tone was fitting.

Mr. Howard nodded, the sort of nod one would use when discussing deaths or difficult legal questions or war. "There are some very fine trees in Essex."

Harry fought back a smile. *Work your magic, Howard.*

"I believe I saw several very exemplary trees when I was last in Essex," a gentleman standing near Athena said. Harry recognized him. Charles Dalforth was a gentleman of some expectations, if not true personal wealth, who was universally regarded as honorable and declared to be a good sort of chap by the members of his club. He would require watching, Harry decided. But Mr. Howard was to be the focus of that evening's undertaking. Mr. Dalforth's eyes met Harry's, a look of amusement in their depths. He, apparently, could see the ridiculousness of Mr. Howard's conversation.

Harry simply raised his eyebrows and allowed his lips to turn up ever so slightly.

Mr. Howard nodded, the space between his eyebrows creasing with thought. "Indeed. We have some very fine elms."

A general nod rippled through the group. Persephone turned toward one of the others gathered nearby and opened her mouth to speak, but Mr. Howard spoke again.

"And birches."

Persephone offered a polite smile.

"Ash."

Harry allowed his eyes to stray to Athena and was not disappointed. She seemed to be fluctuating between confusion and amusement.

"Willow."

All eyes were on Mr. Howard. His rather bland and exceptionally persistent listing of native trees had caught the others off guard.

"Yew."

Athena's eyes met Harry's, and he could no longer hold back his smile. She raised an eyebrow in obvious inquiry, tipping her head slightly in Mr. Howard's direction. Harry managed an almost indiscernible shrug but allowed a small lifting of his eyebrows. Her eyes narrowed slightly. Harry pasted his most innocent expression on his face.

Slowly, beautifully, a smile spread across her mouth, bringing out the mesmerizing dimple he'd discovered at the left of her mouth the first time he'd seen her smile. Harry had to force himself to continue breathing evenly, to prevent any trace of the effect she had on him from showing in his features. Lands, she was beautiful.

"Miss Lancaster." Mr. Howard's voice broke the moment, pulling Athena's still-smiling gaze away from Harry. He immediately felt loss at the severed connection, even as he registered the relief of being able to breathe again. "I see you are enthusiastic about yews."

A flicker of surprise passed over Athena's face, and Harry had to force back his grin once more. "Yews?" Athena repeated. "As in trees?"

"What other yews are there?" Mr. Howard asked quite seriously.

"There are sheep," Mr. Dalforth supplied, a touch of humor barely noticeable in his tone. "Ewes, I believe, can refer to sheep."

"But that is spelled differently," Mr. Howard answered as though puzzling out a very complicated matter.

Mr. Dalforth smiled. "So it is," he said with obvious good humor. He turned to Persephone. "Your Grace." He bowed quite properly. "I believe our hostess is indicating that the second half of tonight's entertainment"—he offered the last word with a note of irony in his voice—"is set to begin. I must reluctantly take my leave, as my mother quite specifically requested I sit beside her this evening."

"One must ever be mindful of one's mother," Persephone replied.

"Indeed," Mr. Dalforth said. "And I was pleased to make your acquaintance, Miss Lancaster," he offered to Athena.

"And I yours, Mr. Dalforth," Athena replied with a smile.

Harry was quick to reassure himself that Athena's smile for *him* had been far broader.

No sooner had Mr. Dalforth slipped from sight than Mr. Howard picked up the discarded topic of only moments earlier. "What other trees are among your favorites, Miss Lancaster?" he asked Athena.

"Well . . . I . . ." Harry fancied he could see her thoughts tumbling in her head as she strove for an answer. "There is a very fine holly tree near the gates to Falstone Castle."

"Holly," Mr. Howard replied, nodding gravely, brow furrowed with contemplation.

"Shall we escort the ladies to their seats?" Harry suggested to Mr. Howard.

His suggestion was taken up with enthusiasm by Mr. Howard, if not by Athena. She cast him a very brief but very loaded glance of surprise. In the end, civility required she accept the arm Mr. Howard offered and endure the ongoing list of trees he continued to belabor as they moved slowly back to the spot she and her sister had occupied during the first part of the evening.

Mr. Howard took his leave of the ladies in the ponderous way Harry had come to expect before making his way back to his own seat. Harry, by virtue of having accompanied the ladies to the Hardfords', had a seat between Athena and her sister and was not obliged to remove himself from their presence.

"Was there a reason, Mr. Windover," Athena whispered over the sounds of the assembly settling in, "for your rather pointed introduction to Mr. Howard?"

She sounded slightly put out. Harry took that as a good sign.

"Did you not like Mr. Howard?" Harry asked.

"It is not a matter of *dis*liking him," Athena replied. "I simply wonder if you had anticipated that I would like him so very much. I have never known you to be so obvious in making Persephone and I known to your friends."

Friend? Mr. Howard hardly fell into that category.

"Am I to assume then, my dear"—Harry kept the endearment light all the while assessing her reaction to it. She seemed not to notice—"that Mr. Howard has not proven the object of your matrimonial searching?"

"I beg your pardon?" Athena replied, her voice a shocked whisper.

"He is, I assure you, both a gentleman and quite eligible. You informed me only last night that those were your only requirements." Harry managed to keep his tone and expression innocent. "I thought you would be pleased to meet the fulfillment of all your hopes and dreams."

"What do you know of my hopes and dreams?" Athena asked, turning her face away from him and toward the pianoforte at the front of the room.

I guarantee I know more of yours than you know of mine. "Again, I remind you of your declarations of not twenty-four hours ago," Harry said aloud, though quietly. "A gentleman who is eligible. I see no way in which Mr. Howard does not meet those requirements. Unless there are other things you desire in a potential suitor of which you have not made me aware."

Athena turned back to look at him, her mouth set in a line of growing annoyance. "I should very much like any suitor for my hand to have more conversation than a ceaseless listing of flora."

"So the man who will win your heart ought to be a gentleman, eligible, *and* conversant." Harry made a show of setting this bit of insight to memory.

"And not be so decidedly serious," Athena added, shaking her head. "I would hope he would improve upon greater acquaintance, but somehow I find myself doubtful. I could not bear the continuing company of a man who was so very grave all the time."

"A gentleman, eligible, conversant, *and* with some degree of lightheartedness." Harry nodded in approval. "Should I find myself in company with such a one, I shall be certain to introduce him to you."

Any response Athena might have made was prevented by the resuming of the musical showcasing common to the *ton*'s musicales.

Harry's mind was already turning. Athena's list had become a little more specific—precisely what he had hoped for. But it was hardly specific enough to prevent a catastrophic misalliance. The question remained: which absolutely essential character trait ought he to convince her of next?

Chapter 4

OBVIOUSLY, IT HAD BEEN A bad idea.

Athena tensed, watching Adam out of the corner of her eye. He was not happy. At all. They were moments from departing for another ball, one Adam had no intention of attending. It had seemed an opportune time for Persephone to bring up a very touchy subject. But it hadn't worked as well as Athena and her sister had hoped.

"Every young lady making her debut must have a come-out ball, Adam," Persephone said quietly but firmly. "And it would be exceptionally badly done of us not to host it for her. You are her guardian, her brother-in-law, her sponsor in society. It falls to us to give Athena her ball."

"I danced with her at Debensham's," Adam replied curtly. "Society will not expect more of me."

Athena was close enough to them in the drawing room to overhear Persephone and Adam's conversation but far enough away to be unnoticed by them. Feeling tense and worried, Athena sat on a straight-backed chair and lightly rubbed her fingers against her forehead, closing her eyes and willing the disagreement to end swiftly. Persephone had been so certain Adam would agree to the ball. Athena didn't want to push him beyond his limit. She had heard of the duke's infamous temper. Though she had not personally been witness to any violence on his part, she did not doubt that he was every bit as harsh as his reputation painted him.

"Do not declare defeat yet," Mr. Windover said quietly from just beside her. He had listened to the proposal of a ball at Falstone House but had not joined the ensuing debate. "Adam did not say no outright. He would have if he were absolutely set against the ball."

"But he is so obviously unhappy about the idea," Athena answered quietly. As always, Mr. Windover's presence was calming. "I don't see how we can ever convince him to agree to it."

She glanced at Mr. Windover. He was smiling as usual. And there was a look in his eyes she had learned to recognize as she'd come to know him better. It was silent laughter, not at anyone's expense, but from an inherent enjoyment of life. He obviously felt himself equal to the task of convincing the society-shunning duke to invite hordes of the Upper Ten-thousand into his home. Athena gave him a look of silent challenge, daring him to live up to the promise in his expression. Harry's smile turned into something resembling both a smirk and a grin.

"You realize, of course, Adam," Mr. Windover interrupted the conversation between husband and wife without the slightest hint of remorse, "you will be obligated to extend an invitation to our esteemed prince when you begin the arduous task of making a guest list."

Adam's head snapped in Mr. Windover's direction, his expression hardened and fiery.

"Mr. Windover," Athena whispered urgently.

"Have some faith, m'dear," Mr. Windover said under his breath. Full voice, he continued addressing Adam. "I, for one, will be waiting on tenterhooks to see if he will attend or not."

"You think the prince would dare refuse the invitation?" Adam threw back.

"Do you wish him to attend?" Mr. Windover asked.

"I would rather walk stark naked through Hyde Park."

"Adam," Persephone scolded, throwing a quick glance in Athena's direction. She probably ought to have been scandalized. But the time she'd spent with her brother-in-law had taught her to not be surprised by anything he might say. Frightened, perhaps, but not surprised.

"And yet if the prince does not attend the ball—" Mr. Windover continued.

"I'll call the ball of mutton out," Adam announced firmly.

"And therein lies the entertainment value," Mr. Windover explained, smiling and leaning back casually in his chair near Athena. "Our prince will receive an invitation he dare not refuse but is terrified to accept."

Adam was silent. And absolutely still. Athena's eyes flicked between everyone in the room. Persephone was watching Adam, her expression hopeful. Mr. Windover wore his usual look of casual amusement. Adam looked intensely thoughtful.

"Georgie was irritatingly rude at the last drawing room," Adam said. By *Georgie,* Athena assumed he meant the prince, though she had never heard him referred to that way.

"Heart-stopping fear can do that to a fellow," Harry observed.

Athena held back a smile.

"The spineless lump of dough deserves a moment of abject humiliation," Adam declared as if insulting one's prince was quite a normal thing for a person to do. "Plan your ball, Persephone," Adam ordered. "But allow *me* to word the royal invitation."

"Let us leave your sister to express her gratitude," Mr. Windover suggested quietly and offered Athena his hand to help her rise. As they passed Adam, Mr. Windover said, "I will see that Miss Lancaster has her wrap and ascertain whether the carriage has been brought around."

"You practically live here, Harry," Adam said tersely. "If I have to listen to the two of you *Mister* and *Miss* each other for the rest of the Little Season, one or the other of you is not going to live to see Christmas."

Athena tensed. But Mr. Windover laughed. "So for our health, if nothing else, we should endeavor to be on a Christian-name basis in family settings."

"There is no *endeavor* about it," Adam said. "You will do so."

"But you never have called me out, Adam," Harry answered. "And you have promised to do so many times."

"Do not tempt me."

"How shall I spend my excessive free time if I abandon one of my favorite hobbies?"

Adam's eyes narrowed. Athena tugged on Mr. Windover's arm, concerned that he'd finally pushed Adam too far.

"Harry, do step out," Persephone insisted. "I have no desire to bid my husband farewell with you in the room offering a running commentary."

Mr. Windover laughed his infectious chuckle and led Athena from the room. The door was firmly closed behind them.

"They are a little nauseating, aren't they?" Mr. Windover said.

"I do not understand them," Athena confessed. "Adam is so surly and unapproachable, and Persephone is so obviously in love with him."

"*Surly and unapproachable.*" He seemed to be weighing her word choice. "I do believe that is the tamest set of descriptors I have ever heard attached to Adam's name."

Which brought to mind another thing that had puzzled Athena. "Does Adam often refer to our prince as *Georgie*?"

"Only when Adam is particularly cross with him," Mr. Windover answered with another characteristic laugh. "It was that nickname that brought about the aborted duel I told you of recently."

"Indeed?" Athena was intrigued.

"Adam called the prince *Georgie*—to his face—at a rather important gathering of society's most elite. It was, of course, a monumental embarrassment to His Royal Highness, and he said something rather regrettable to Adam. It was that comment which led to Adam's issuing a challenge."

"Good heavens," Athena said. "What did the prince say? It must have been something drastic to warrant calling out the heir to the throne."

Mr. Windover smiled at her, that twinkle of devilment in his eyes Athena was beginning to realize was commonplace for him. "You are anticipating an insult of the highest magnitude, are you not?"

Athena smiled back at him.

"Perhaps you are envisioning a set of words so base or horrendous that I would hesitate to repeat them in the company of a genteel young lady such as yourself."

"Except your tone tells me such an assumption would not be entirely correct."

"Very wise, Athena—and, I assure you, I am using your Christian name at the insistence of your guardian, not because I am a presumptuous, ill-mannered lout."

"Are you saying that you *are* a presumptuous, ill-mannered lout—just not in this particular instance?"

He laughed at that show of wit, something Athena appreciated. Evander had always been her companion in jests and intellectual swordplay. How she'd missed him in the years since he'd gone to sea. And how deeply she'd mourned his death in battle only a year earlier. She'd never thought to find another who enjoyed the same type of interaction.

"Perhaps you will be willing to forgive this ill-mannered lout when you consider the fact that I quite single-handedly secured Adam's blessing for your come-out ball," Mr. Windover said. "That was rather miraculous of me, don't you think?"

"I still do not understand how you managed that, Mr. Windover." Athena shook her head at the recollection. It had seemed a lost cause before he had completely turned the situation around.

"Please call me Harry when we are in private," he replied. "I would hate for Adam to think we have ignored his dictate. He can be a little testy when he feels his authority is underestimated."

Athena laughed lightly, as she was sure Mr. Windover, Harry, intended her to.

"Shall I explain to you the secret to Adam, then?" Harry smiled conspiratorially. "This is a great deal of power to trust to someone so young."

"I am nineteen years old, sir," Athena informed him, her tone of indignation as obviously feigned as his exaggerated air of condescension.

"An ancient, to be sure."

"If I am an ancient, you must be an artifact."

"I do have nine years more in my dish than you do," Harry replied.

"Decrepit." Athena laughed.

"I had better divulge my closely guarded secret before the effects of old age wipe it from my undependable memory," Harry said. "Though you may not credit it, Adam and Persephone are almost disgustingly enamored of one another. For Adam's part, he would do absolutely anything for his wife. *Anything.* But having lived his life dictating every facet of his existence and catering to no one's whims or wishes, he struggles to allow himself to act on his desire to please her. The Infamous Duke of Kielder never gives an inch, never breaks from routine. The key to securing his cooperation lies in giving him a reason to change his plans or inclinations that does not compromise his formidable reputation."

"You invent menacing excuses for him to do completely ordinary things?"

"They aren't excuses," Harry replied. "They are legitimate reasons why someone like Adam would do something generally considered out of character for him."

"Like allowing his wife to throw a ball?"

"Precisely," Harry answered. "He would never deny her anything she truly wished for. Adam loves her far too much to disappoint her if it is in his power to do otherwise. But he struggles with it still. So I regularly rack my brain composing sufficiently treacherous reasons for him to make his wife happy."

Athena shook her head as she thought through Harry's explanation. "And an opportunity to discommode His Royal Highness is treacherous enough?"

"Barely."

"Good heavens." She laughed, partly out of amusement but mostly out of amazement.

"The carriage is ready, Mr. Windover," the butler informed them, holding open the front door as a maid slipped a heavy shawl around Athena's shoulders.

"Excellent." Persephone's voice rang behind them. She glided past, making her way outside, her cheeks flushed and a broad smile on her face.

Following behind with her arm through Harry's, Athena was quick to push from her mind the reason for her sister's blush and grin. It was difficult to fathom the fearsome Duke of Kielder doing something as emotional and tender as kissing his wife.

"Your curiosity is sadly lacking, Athena," Harry said.

"Curiosity?" About Their Graces' private moment? Surely that was not what he meant.

"Do you not have any desire to know what it was our unfortunate prince said to the terrifying duke to warrant an invitation to meet on the grass?"

Athena smiled back at him. "I cannot even imagine something drastic enough to warrant such an occurrence."

"It was inexcusable," Harry said, but there was a chuckle behind the words. "His Royal Highness, after hearing himself called *Georgie,* locked eyes with Adam and said, 'How dare you, Kielder?' And Adam took it upon himself to assure the prince that he dared at whatever time and place His Highness should choose and by whatever means he decided upon. He further advised our prince to secure a very competent surgeon in the off-chance that Adam's aim was not as true as usual."

"Meaning, of course, that Adam might accidentally shoot His Royal Highness."

"No," Harry said. "That Adam might accidentally *not kill* His Royal Highness and that he would thus need a surgeon. Adam does not believe in deloping; regardless of his opponent, he would never intentionally miss. Every gentleman knows as much."

Athena felt her eyes widen. Adam had, essentially, threatened to kill a member of the royal family. "Did you not say the prince apologized to Adam?"

"Instantaneously."

Athena stopped at the carriage door and turned back to look at Harry. "Would Adam have shot the prince if they had met on the field of honor?"

"No," Harry smiled reassuringly. "But the prince was not so certain, and Adam had no intention of clarifying that point."

"So the prince wouldn't risk it?"

"There are some risks that are not worth taking," Harry answered.

"Is there anything you will not risk where Adam is concerned?" Athena doubted it.

But Harry didn't answer. He simply handed her up and kept his peace as they traveled toward the night's destination.

Chapter 5

WITH ADAM CONSPICUOUSLY ABSENT, ATHENA was unques-
tionably the belle of the ball. The gentlemen were
swarming. And if the eager looks she was receiving from all and
sundry were any indication, Athena's reign as the Diamond of
the Little Season would be short-lived. She would be married
before Christmas at the rate she was collecting swains.

Harry made a concerted effort not to think about Athena's
success as he made his way around the ballroom. There was one
gentleman in particular to whom he was anxious to introduce
Athena. *Eligible, a gentleman, conversant, and at least minimally
lighthearted.* Those were Athena's only requirements, to date. It
certainly was not enough to prevent disaster.

He shook his head at himself. When had he taken on the
role of deliverer from self-created disasters?

"Miss Lancaster certainly seems to have been declared a peerless diamond." Mr. Charles Dalforth spoke from beside Harry,
sipping casually from a champagne flute.

"I was only just thinking precisely the same thing," Harry
admitted. He had grudgingly conceded that Dalforth did,
indeed, have a great deal to recommend himself after speaking
with him a handful of times since the Hardfords' musicale.
And though Harry had spent the better part of an afternoon
attempting to find Dalforth's fatal flaw, he had not discovered

anything to discredit the gentleman, Harry's junior by not more than two or three years.

"It will be enlightening, however, to see how many of her eager admirers desert the field when His Grace of Kielder makes another appearance," Dalforth observed.

Harry had to smile at that. "I predict a mass disappearance."

Dalforth chuckled. "Every one of Her Grace's sisters will, I believe, be required to marry gentlemen who are almost ridiculously courageous. Or, at the very least, do not feel the usual pull of self-preservation."

Courageous. Harry silently thanked Dalforth. It was another character trait Athena ought to be searching for. Not simply because a cowardly beau would never summon the courage to approach Adam to ask for her hand, but, more importantly, because a lily-livered husband would inevitably ostracize Athena from her family. Adam had no patience with cowards and would make the hypothetical gentleman excessively uncomfortable whenever they were in company. In the end, it would mean estrangement between Athena and her sisters.

"Miss Lancaster is dancing with Mr. Howard," Dalforth said, motioning subtly toward the dance floor with his chin. "I do not believe she will thank you for that introduction, Windover." Dalforth was smiling amusedly.

Harry laughed in spite of himself. "I did not make the introduction in order to secure her gratitude."

Dalforth turned an inquisitive glance on Harry. "You wished to upset her?" he asked, censure lacing his tone.

"Not at all," Harry reassured him. Apparently Dalforth considered himself something of a protector where Athena was concerned. Harry didn't like that thought one bit. "The young lady is quite inexperienced with the world," Harry explained, "and knows little of people and characters. I believe she will benefit from knowing a variety of gentlemen, so she can make a more informed decision when the time comes to bestow her affections."

"And you felt she would benefit from making the acquaintance of an absolute bore?" Dalforth chuckled, his good humor apparently restored.

Harry smiled. "So she would come to appreciate the importance of a gentleman who *does* have some of her same interests."

"Or any interests at all," Dalforth added, laughter bubbling just below the surface. "Mr. Howard is something of a dull dog, but he is harmless."

"Precisely," Harry answered, feeling an unasked-for rapport with the gentleman.

"You seem to fit very naturally into the role of avuncular guide."

Avuncular? The irony of that word choice was enormous. His feelings for Athena were as far from that of a fond uncle as seemingly possible. But Dalforth's words proved Harry was putting a convincing face on his interactions with her.

His eyes followed Athena as she and Mr. Howard passed down the line of dancers in their set. The look of confused surprise most people wore around Howard momentarily crossed her features, and Harry wondered what the man had said to bring that look to her face. Perhaps another tree? Harry smiled at the thought.

Howard was making more than one point on Harry's behalf. Being conversant was all well and good. But the ability to engage in conversation that was intellectual on even a minimal level was far preferable. Athena, Harry was certain, was beginning to see that.

Out of the corner of his eye, Harry spotted the very person he'd been on the lookout for all evening. Mr. Cameron Peterbrook met all of Athena's expressed requirements. As the younger son of a viscount, he was certainly a gentleman. He was unattached and socially acceptable and, therefore, eligible. Harry knew he was reasonably intelligent, not averse to conversation, and not overly serious. Everything Athena could possibly wish for, it would seem.

Harry held back a mischievous grin and strode across the ballroom.

* * *

Harry appeared to be in a good mood. Not that Athena had ever seen him in anything but good spirits. He simply seemed to be smiling even more than usual. Perhaps, she thought to herself, he was simply happy for her. This ball—the second of her Season—had been a far better experience than her first.

Just as he had at the Debensham's, Harry had claimed her supper dance and was, therefore, accompanying her and Persephone to the supper room. "Thank you, Mr. Windover," Athena said as he laid her plate in front of her. Formality was needed in a social setting unless their voices were lowered enough not to be overheard. "Most especially for the macaroons." She smiled.

"I seem to remember they are a favorite of yours," Harry replied, his eyes laughing. "Artemis, you will recall, has predicted you will die of overindulgence in macaroons before you reach the age of twenty-five."

Athena and Persephone both laughed at the memory of their youngest sister's scold. Artemis, at nine, was far too outspoken for her own good. But she was such an absolutely darling little girl that one could not possibly hold anything she said against her.

"Artemis will certainly run us all a merry chase over the next ten years or more." Persephone smiled, shaking her head in amusement.

They all smiled at the truth of that statement and began partaking of the delicacies provided by their hostess.

"Windover, old chap, here you are," a voice drawled, pulling Athena's attention from her supper. A gentleman stood beside their table, one hip cocked out, hand fisted and resting against it, a self-satisfied smile on his face. He was dressed to absolute perfection, not a single wrinkle marring his impeccably tailored black jacket. His almost blindingly white cravat was so symmetrical it might very well have been carved by the hand of a sculpting master. And there was absolutely no denying the gentleman was astoundingly handsome.

"Ah, Peterbrook," Harry replied, smiling up at the stranger. "Well met. Well met. Your Grace," Harry turned toward Persephone, "may I present to you Mr. Peterbrook of Caddelford in Lancashire." Persephone inclined her head ever so slightly. She was remarkably good at being a lofty duchess. Athena nearly always had to fight a smile when Persephone slipped on her social mask. "Peterbrook, might I make known to you Her Grace, the Duchess of Kielder."

They exchanged the expected pleasantries after which Persephone introduced Athena and Mr. Peterbrook to one another. Harry then invited Mr. Peterbrook to join them, an invitation Mr. Peterbrook accepted with a dashing smile. After Mr. Howard's discussion of the finer points of elms—which took the better part of the country dance he'd engaged Athena's hand for, despite his having only spoken half a dozen times—Athena was anxious for a real conversation. Despite her original intention not to create a checklist for husband requirements, she was finding herself compiling one. The ability to converse was certainly high on the list. And, though she hadn't considered it consciously before, she found herself adding "handsome" to her requirements as well.

"Weston, isn't it?" Harry asked Mr. Peterbrook, inclining his head in the approximate direction of Mr. Peterbrook's evening jacket.

"Most certainly," Mr. Peterbrook replied, an eyebrow raised as if in shock at the question. "You certainly didn't suppose I had patronized an inferior tailor. Did you?" Again, the shock.

"Not at all," Harry reassured him with a smile. "I was simply confirming what I knew to be a certainty."

"A gentleman cannot possibly underestimate the importance of a competent tailor," Mr. Peterbrook informed them with an air of authority.

"Is that so?" Harry replied. Athena glanced at him, something in his tone striking her as strange. The interest she heard in his voice seemed too great to be real, and yet she didn't detect laughter behind it. That, alone, was unusual for Harry.

"Indeed." Mr. Peterbrook stared across the table at Harry, his expression shifting from surprise to something resembling pity. "If one is to look one's best, which is, as we know all, entirely essential, the fit of one's coat is paramount."

"I do not believe that rule can be applied universally, Peterbrook," Harry answered, a smile touching the very corner of his mouth. "I daresay, for a lady, the fit of her jacket is not a consideration."

Athena held back a laugh. Harry had found a hole in Mr. Peterbrook's reasoning quite immediately. Ladies did not, after all, wear the formal jackets that men did.

"But the fit of *our* jackets would, most certainly, be taken into consideration by ladies of taste and refinement," Mr. Peterbrook replied. "An ill-fitting jacket or a poorly tied cravat or a inferiorly shod foot could spell social disaster for one less well-versed in such things as I." He smiled that devastating smile Athena had first noticed as he'd taken his seat at their table.

"You are considered something of a leader in the world of gentlemen's fashions," Harry acknowledged.

"Quite right," Mr. Peterbrook answered. "It is one of the few distinctions of which a gentleman may be truly proud."

"Indeed?" Athena replied, unable to entirely hide the disbelief in her voice.

Mr. Peterbrook smiled at her as if she had wholeheartedly concurred with him.

"I believe the Duke of Kielder is considered to be a gentleman of significant influence in Parliament," Athena said. "Do you not consider that a distinction of which he might be proud?"

Athena thought she saw Harry force back a smile but did not look away from Mr. Peterbrook long enough to know for sure.

"As His Grace is always quite well-togged, being influential in the government while impressively attired could, I suppose, be considered an accomplishment worth noting. Though, one cannot overlook the fact that he could never be considered handsome."

"You place a great deal of importance upon appearances, Mr. Peterbrook." Anyone who truly knew Persephone would have recognized the ice in her tone. Adam's face was badly scarred during his childhood, which was, no doubt, the reason behind Mr. Peterbrook's declaration of Adam as not handsome. Persephone would never take such a comment lightly. But Mr. Peterbrook, as Athena was coming to expect was usual for him, took Persephone's words as a compliment.

"What could possibly be more important, Your Grace?" he asked with a broad and probably well-rehearsed smile.

The man was as shallow as a puddle. *What could be more important than appearances?* Could he actually believe that? It very much seemed he did.

"And I further feel," Mr. Peterbrook continued, oblivious to the lack of enthusiasm among his companions, "that when one is blessed with excessively good looks"—another flashing white smile—"one is, not to put it too lightly, *required* to complement such physical beauty with those things that will enhance the nearly flawless handiwork of nature."

"Nearly flawless?" Persephone repeated, the ice in her tone joined by a hint of barely repressed laughter.

"So I have been told." Mr. Peterbrook straightened his unwrinkled sleeve.

Athena spoke, almost as if she could not help herself, as if the absurdity of what Mr. Peterbrook was saying absolutely forced her to seek some degree of understanding. "You must have an opinion, then, of who shares with you the distinction of being 'nearly flawless.'"

"There are many," he replied, "who come close."

"But do not equal your level of . . ." Athena searched for the right word.

"Perfection," Mr. Peterbrook supplied without a hint of hesitation.

"Is there no one, sir, who can equal you, then?" Athena asked, beginning to feel her dislike of Mr. Peterbrook's character surpassing her admiration for his very handsome countenance.

Mr. Peterbrook's gaze turned speculative and evaluative. Athena stiffened under his gaze, knowing she was being sized up. "Miss Lancaster," he said, approval in his tone, "should you acquire a carriage dress of green in a shade matching that of your eyes, I daresay I would not be at all ashamed to be seen riding out with you. Indeed, I do believe that should we be seen together—you in green and I in the deep blue that so complements my own peerless eyes—we should be considered quite a handsome couple. And being in my company could only raise your appeal in the eyes of all who see us together."

Athena had no idea whether to thank the man or to be affronted. As it was, she simply sat, mute and confused, as Mr. Peterbrook smiled approvingly.

"You certainly have a very unique way of bestowing a compliment, Mr. Peterbrook," Persephone observed in a tone that was not at all complimentary.

"I have often been told so," Mr. Peterbrook replied, his smile never slipping.

"Knowing your penchant for maintaining a flawless appearance," Harry entered the conversation for the first time in some minutes, "I feel it imperative that I inform you that you seem to have acquired a small dollop of some sauce or another on your cuff."

A look of horror passed over Mr. Peterbrook's face as he searched his cuff and found the offending spot. With speed that bordered on incivility, Mr. Peterbrook rose, offered the expected bows, and excused himself.

After a moment of stunned silence had passed, Persephone spoke. "Adam will be so pleased to know he is considered 'well-togged.'"

Her tone was perfectly serious, but Athena and Harry both laughed out loud. Adam could care less what any person thought of his clothing.

"Come to think of it, though, I had best not mention the rest of Mr. Peterbrook's evaluation to my tempestuous husband," Persephone added. "He is not likely to appreciate being told he could never be considered handsome, however untrue such an evaluation might be."

"It is, apparently, entirely true in Mr. Peterbrook's estimable opinion," Harry replied.

"*Estimable?*" Athena objected, though she kept her voice too low to carry beyond their small group. "I do not care how well his tailor turns him out, I do not place any confidence in that man's evaluation of any person. Mr. Peterbrook is without a doubt the most shallow, self-absorbed individual I have ever had the misfortune to meet."

"Am I to assume he will not be in the running for your hand, Athena?" Harry asked, leaning closer to her and speaking so softly she could barely make out his words.

"How could you think otherwise?" Athena replied, matching his volume.

"He is a gentleman, I assure you, and entirely eligible. And, you must admit, has the ability to hold up his end of a conversation. He is also not overly somber." Harry shrugged slightly. "Those were, I understood, your only specific requirements in a suitor."

"Well, you may add 'some depth of character' and 'a healthy dose of humility' to that list, Mr. Windover," Athena answered, pursing her lips. Drat the man, he was practically forcing an unromantic list-making on her.

"Mr. Windover?" Harry repeated. "Are you upset with me?"

She sighed. "No. I simply find I do not very much care for your friends," Athena answered, thinking of Mr. Howard as well as Mr. Peterbrook.

"Howard and Peterbrook are more acquaintances than friends," Harry said as if reading her thoughts. "Of course, if you would prefer I not introduce you to the gentlemen I know . . ."

"No," Athena reassured him. How was she ever to find the man of her dreams if she never met anyone? "I appreciate your helping Adam and Persephone with my Season, truly I do."

"It is my pleasure," he replied, but something in his tone sounded almost regretful.

"Dare I hope you will eventually introduce me to a gentleman who *doesn't* have a glaringly lacking character?"

His reply sounded almost like "Don't hold your breath." But such a response would not make sense, so Athena dismissed the possibility.

A gentleman who is eligible, conversant, lighthearted, possessing some depth of character, and who is not self-absorbed and conceited. Surely that was not too much to ask for. The romantic in her still objected to the cold and calculating nature of a list, but Athena's logical side was finding it remarkably beneficial.

Chapter 6

HARRY WAS WHISTLING AS HE walked into Adam's book room. Adam hated when Harry whistled. And though it was difficult to do so while fighting a grin, Harry took the opportunity to whistle a jaunty tune once in a while when Adam was certain to overhear.

Adam was rolling his eyes as Harry dropped into his usual wingback armchair just to the side of Adam's imposing desk. Harry had long ago refused to sit in the abnormally low straight-back chair that sat directly across from Adam. It was a place meant to inspire a feeling of inferiority and discomfort to its occupant. Harry would really rather not.

"Your message sounded urgent," Harry said casually. In all reality he was excessively curious. *Falstone House. Now.* That was the extent of Adam's scrawled note. The curtness of it meant Adam was either angry or annoyed. Harry preferred annoyed—it was a far less tricky state of mind to navigate. Adam was a touch too unpredictable when he was truly angry.

"And yet," Adam said, "you took more than an hour to arrive."

The irritation in Adam's tone was reassuring. "It didn't sound *that* urgent," Harry replied, leaning back in his chair, presenting the very picture of unconcerned relaxation.

"A gentleman of sense would have found any correspondence from me urgent to the point of panic."

"The fact that I am so obviously something of a flat must really burn your spleen," Harry observed.

"Cut the cant, Harry." That was Adam's usual reply to Harry's use of slang. Adam disliked slang as much as whistling. Probably more. "I am out of patience with you as it is."

"And what sin do you have to lay at my door this time?" Harry asked with a chuckle he didn't bother to hide. He had become something of an expert on Adam Boyce over the years, learning to read his expressions and tones as easily as he read words on a paper. It was true, Adam was certainly annoyed with Harry. But his disgruntled feelings didn't go beyond that. There was no true anger, simply irritation.

Adam raised an eyebrow, face stern, mouth a thin line of disapproval. He held up a sheet of paper, its writing visible but not legible from a distance, folded in a way that proclaimed it a piece of correspondence.

Odd. Harry couldn't immediately identify what a letter could contain that would gain him Adam's ire. Nor could he guess from whom the letter might have come.

Quite suddenly, Adam was not alone at his desk. A girl, small for her age with her dark hair pulled back in two long plaits, deep-brown eyes contrasting against her pale face, stood beside Adam, her gaze darting between the two men. Daphne, Athena's twelve-year-old sister, had a way of moving about the house in such absolute silence that one never anticipated her arrival in a room.

Harry smiled at her, as he always did when they were in company with one another. Her cheeks pinked as usual. But to Harry's surprise, instead of the posture of bashful discomfort she had assumed in the past, Daphne moved closer to Adam, curling into his side. Adam reached out to his silent sister-in-law and wrapped his arm around her slim shoulders, actually pulling her closer to him, remaining seated. Harry stared in astonished disbelief. This was not the prickly, unapproachable Adam Boyce he knew.

"What is it, Daphne?" Adam asked, every trace of annoyance gone from his tone. Harry thought Adam even almost smiled.

"I wanted to come sit with you," she answered, her voice so quiet Harry could barely make out her words. Her eyes darted to him for a moment before returning to gaze at her clasped hands, hanging in front of her. "It is four o'clock. As always."

"Yes, but Mr. Windover is here an hour late," Adam replied.

"And your business is such that I cannot remain," Daphne stated. On the few occasions Harry had interacted with Daphne, he had been impressed by her maturity and intelligence. For a girl who was little more than a child, she had a remarkably sharp mind.

"I am afraid not," Adam replied.

Daphne nodded, her features taking on a look of neutrality that, when she happened to glance briefly in Harry's direction, was belied by the disappointment he saw in her eyes. Did this unlikely pair truly spend afternoons regularly in one another's company? Who had instigated the arrangement—somehow Harry couldn't picture either party doing so. Adam was too gruff and preferred isolation. Daphne was too reserved.

Harry heard Daphne take an oddly shaky breath in the moment before he realized her eyes had turned uncomfortably bright, and her chin was wobbling ever so slightly.

"Daphne." Adam's gentle rebuke broke into the silence. "You know the rules."

She nodded. "No crying," she whispered.

"Precisely. Now I will be in Lords tomorrow but should have time the day after for our usual afternoon discussion," Adam said.

Daphne looked up at Adam, brows creased in concentration. "What if *he* comes back?" she asked, nodding her head toward Harry as she emphasized *he*.

"I'll throw him out." Adam shrugged.

Daphne smiled up at her brother-in-law, putting Harry firmly in mind of her older sister, except that Athena's hair was golden and curly, her eyes a startling shade of green. Daphne, other than the creamy pale of her skin, had much darker coloring. Their smiles, however, were the same—down to the single dimple near the left corner of her mouth.

Even more shocking, Adam smiled back at her. He never smiled at anyone. Harry was certain it was partly the result of self-consciousness. Adam's facial scars made his smiles uneven and puckered. The remaining reason was his disgruntled nature. Adam very seldom found a reason to smile.

As silently as she had entered, Daphne left the book room. Without a word of explanation for his complete character shift in the presence of his young sister-in-law, Adam took hold of the letter he'd held aloft a moment before Daphne's arrival and held it up once more, his eyes focused again on Harry. The message was obvious. Adam would not discuss Daphne.

"Ah, yes, the mysterious letter," Harry said, shaking off his lingering confusion over the interaction he'd just watched.

"Mr. George Howard," Adam said, his words once again clipped and impatient.

With that, Harry burst out laughing.

Adam raised an eyebrow, his expression stern.

"What on earth was he writing about?" Harry managed.

"You tell me, Harry. You are supposed to be sorting through the suitors so I am not bothered by them."

"Suitors?" Harry grinned. "Is the man writing you love letters?"

Adam didn't look amused. "He has written to request permission to court Athena."

"Written?" Harry chuckled. "Isn't that sort of thing usually done in person?"

Adam's eyes dropped to the letter, and he began reading with the same tone of mocking annoyance he used when reading letters from his cousin and heir-presumptive—a man whose intelligence and bravery Adam found entirely lacking. "'Miss Lancaster likes trees. I like trees. It seems we would suit. But only if Your Grace will permit it. I would rather not be shot, so I am asking from a distance.'" Adam dropped the letter onto his desk and shook his head in obvious disapproval. "Imbecile. As if I couldn't shoot him from a distance as easily as I could in my own home."

But Harry was still too diverted by Mr. Howard's reasoning to find Adam's words as amusing as he usually did. *I like trees.* How very fitting it was as a declaration from that particular gentleman.

"What are Athena's feelings regarding this Mr. Howard?" Adam said, phrasing his inquiry as if to indicate he was unfamiliar with Howard, when Harry knew that Adam was perfectly aware of who he was. "Will I need to dispose of him quietly to spare her sensibilities, or does she possess enough intelligence to have already written him off?"

"What do you plan to do if she has no feelings for the unfortunate man?" Harry asked, smiling broadly. "The gibbet is too far away, after all."

"The man practically requested that I shoot him," Adam answered. Anyone who did not know Adam as well as Harry did would never have known the infamous duke actually had no intention of shooting Mr. Howard.

"Well, then, as sorry as this makes me for Mr. Howard, I must truthfully tell you that, far from ruing his loss from her court of admirers, Athena would probably be grateful for your interference."

"So she has not fallen for whatever well-hidden charms the man might possess?" Adam asked.

"Not remotely."

"Then why am *I* dealing with him?" Adam demanded. "You are supposed to be sorting all this out and leaving me out of it."

"I confess I hadn't anticipated a letter," Harry said, barely managing not to chuckle. "And I cannot prevent others from trying the same approach."

"I'll pack her up and leave Town," Adam informed him, a promise blatant in his tone.

It was a tempting prospect. If Athena was not in London making her bows to society, she would not be snatched up, and he, Harry, would not have to endure losing her. But Athena, he knew, would be devastated. As much as seeing her married to another would pain him, he could not bring himself to be party to anything that would so thoroughly disappoint her.

"Perhaps I ought to subtly spread word around the clubs that the Duke of Kielder will not endure impertinent letters from prospective suitors for the hand of his sister-in-law." Harry smiled amusedly. It would not be the first time he had started whispered warnings amongst the gentlemen of society. He liked to think he'd saved many a rash man from the heart-stopping experience of finding himself on the wrong side of His Grace, the Dangerous Duke of Kielder.

Adam nodded. "But not subtly."

"Not subtly. I shall be direct and obvious and will even manage to look pale with fright. The entire *ton* will be too afraid to so much as send you an invitation let alone any actual correspondence."

Adam gave him a look clearly communicating that for all of society to be so entirely overcome with fear would hardly be disappointing.

"Anything else I ought to warn our fellow men about where Athena is concerned?" Harry chuckled.

"Impertinence is annoying but endurable. However, I will not countenance fortune hunters," Adam said. "I can practically smell them coming out of the sewers every time her name comes up. The size of her dowry is well-known. I will not have her snatched up by some pathetic excuse for a man who needs her money like Mr. Howard obviously needed a competent tutor. Let the gentlemen know I have certain standards where a suitor's bank account is concerned."

No glib comment came to mind. It was a directive. Adam had just expressly forbade any gentleman lacking in funds from courting Athena. Harry was officially and inarguably ineligible.

"Oh, dear. This appears to be a very serious discussion." Persephone was standing in the doorway smiling.

"Harry is causing trouble," Adam replied.

"For you as well?" Persephone said, stepping inside and looking on the verge of laughter. "Harry seems to have made quite a handful of enemies in this house today."

"Who else is upset with him?" Adam asked, all outward appearance indicating he was entirely serious. Only the slightest hint of amusement existed in his voice.

Persephone crossed to the desk, tapping her lower lip with her finger as if thinking. Her eyes were twinkling mischievously. "Daphne is apparently put out over what she called Harry's 'shocking lack of punctuality.'" Harry was certain Adam almost laughed. "Artemis is upset because Daphne is back in the nursery, and she was 'absolutely depending' on an hour without her sister. Athena is looking daggers at this very moment and muttering about the unthinkable punishments she plans to heap on Harry's head." She gave Harry a pointed look that was both laughing and entertained.

"Why is Athena upset with me?" Harry asked, not nearly as diverted as he had been by the younger girls' complaints.

"I leave it to you to find out."

"Unfair," Harry complained with a smile.

"But far more enjoyable."

"For *you*."

"Precisely."

"And are you upset with Harry as well?" Adam asked Persephone.

"At the moment I am quite put out with him." But Persephone's smile had only grown.

"And why is that?" Adam asked.

Persephone sat on the edge of Adam's desk, facing him, and reached out one hand to lightly brush a tuft of hair from his face. Persephone's hand trailed down Adam's face to rest along his jaw, her smile turning softer and far too intimate for Harry's comfort.

"Harry," Adam said authoritatively.

"Yes, Adam," Harry said.

"Get out."

Harry laughed and rose from his seat, moving quickly to the door. He glanced back before stepping out of the room only to be greeted with the sight of Adam pulling Persephone into his arms. *Lucky dog.*

Adam was married to his lady love. Harry was, apparently, in trouble with his.

Chapter 7

LAWS! SHE WAS A VISION. There was something almost painful about seeing Athena, the glow from the windows turning her golden halo of curls molten in the early evening sunlight. She possessed a figure any woman would envy and a breathtakingly beautiful countenance. Harry was certain she'd received compliments from more men than she could even remember. He couldn't help wondering what her impression was of him. He didn't consider himself anything out of the ordinary. His hair was neither light nor dark, his eyes an indifferent shade of blue. While a penchant for riding Adam's vast assortment of horses and the necessity of walking whenever his friend's stables were not convenient kept Harry in good physical shape, he doubted his build inspired any of the sighs and longing looks he'd seen directed toward the more sporting members of the Corinthian set.

He must have made some noise passing through the threshold to the drawing room. Athena spun around, her gaze pulled from the scene outside the windows and resting on him. Only a moment was required to register the fact that he had, indeed, found himself in the suds with the usually affable light of his life. The look on her face was decidedly laced with pique. But what on earth had he done?

"Good afternoon, Athena," he greeted warily, approaching slowly and watching her expression for any indication of the reason she was upset with him. No clues were forthcoming.

"Is it?" she asked peevishly.

"A good afternoon?"

She crossed her arms in front of her and watched him, lips pursed. Harry found it necessary to clear his throat. Even his cravat had grown uncomfortably snug. Lud, he needed to find out what he'd done to warrant such a look of reproach. He was discovering that having Athena upset with him was remarkably distressing.

"It is certainly not a good afternoon if you are upset with me," he admitted, moving closer to where she stood glaring at him. Some of Athena's aggravation seemed to slip from her posture, though she did not yet look happy with him. He'd much rather see Athena smile at him than scowl. "Dare I ask what infraction I find myself guilty of committing, or have I further condemned myself by admitting that I do not know the reason for the black looks I am receiving?"

The slightest twitch of a smile tugged at Athena's mouth, and Harry felt himself truly breathing for the first time since entering the room. Perhaps he was to be forgiven, after all.

"I have just endured the most horrendous drive through Hyde Park imaginable," Athena said and gave him a look so pointed that it was obviously meant to be a thorough enough explanation.

"And I am in trouble because *I* was not the one driving you?" Harry asked, using a teasing tone to cover the fact that he genuinely hoped that was the reason.

"I would have far preferred being with you," she confessed, looking as though she was reluctant to say something flattering while she was determined to be upset with him.

"Do you wish to talk about it?" Harry asked. "I have been told I am a remarkably good listener."

He heard Athena sigh and watched as her shoulders slumped. Harry held his hand out to indicate she should sit on the sofa.

He felt his lungs catch in his chest when she slipped her hand in his as she came to his side. Harry wrapped his fingers around hers and walked with her to the sofa. He breathed in the scent of her, the familiar aroma of violets, as he waited for her to speak. He allowed her to sit before reluctantly releasing her hand and sitting in a nearby chair. As much as he would have preferred to sit beside her on the sofa, he knew he did not have that right. He was pushing the bounds of propriety as it was, being alone with her in the drawing room, never mind that the door was left quite widely ajar.

"It was essentially torturous," Athena said with a shrug that wasn't nearly as unconcerned as she probably hoped it to appear.

"With whom did you drive out?" That proved to be the wrong question. Athena pierced him with another look of frustration.

"Mr. Peterbrook," she replied, words tight and accusatory.

"I can certainly understand your displeasure at spending the length of a drive with him," Harry answered, not bothering to hide his confusion. "But how is it that I have earned your wrath over Mr. Peterbrook's obvious lack of address?"

"You introduced him to me," she replied, her tone suggesting such a connection should have been obvious.

"I also introduced you to Mr. Howard," Harry pointed out with a chuckle.

"I know," she replied. "Do you not know any gentlemen who are desirable companions?"

None that you are going to meet. "Perhaps you should tell me precisely what Mr. Peterbrook did that was so distressing so I can be sure to introduce you to gentlemen in the future who are unlikely to commit those same infractions." *They will simply do other obnoxious things.*

"Did you know that Mr. Peterbrook owns twenty-three different Weston coats?" Athena asked, her tone of excitement theatrical in its exaggeration. "Five of them are black. Six are blue, but, apparently, vastly different shades of blue. Would you like to know about his footwear?"

"Did you discuss anything other than his wardrobe?" Harry asked.

Finally a smile broke through Athena's stormy countenance but not broadly enough for that devastating dimple to make an appearance. "He did eventually veer into the myriad compliments paid to him by arbiters of fashion, as well as the precise mixture his valet uses to achieve the enviable shine to the boots that Mr. Peterbrook is, apparently, quite well-known for."

"Did he discuss anything other than himself?"

"At one point he informed me that my pale blue carriage dress was not overly offensive to his aesthetic sensibilities," Athena replied, shaking her head in apparent disbelief but still smiling. "Though he could not understand why I had agreed to drive out with him if I did not, in fact, have a green carriage dress as he required."

"How insufferably pompous."

"I informed him that I only agreed to drive out with him because I could not think of a way to refuse that would not have been unforgivably rude," Athena informed him. "And that, had he not asked me in a room full of people whose opinions matter to me, I should have turned him down regardless."

"You said that to him?" Harry was impressed. He knew Persephone was pluck to the backbone but hadn't realized Athena had quite so much steel in her.

"For all the good it did." She waved a hand dismissively. "Either he wasn't listening or he didn't understand or simply refused to believe that his invitation had not been eagerly accepted."

"I would vote for the last possibility." Harry chuckled. "Peterbrook's opinion of himself is far too high to admit any kind of rejection."

"It was a very long carriage ride." Athena sighed.

An invitation hovered on Harry's lips. How he would enjoy taking her for a jaunt through the park, absorbing the delight of her company, inhaling the scent of violets that followed her wherever she went. But he did not own a single carriage. He had a horse but didn't dare risk spoiling it for riding by hitching it to a conveyance. And there was something decidedly lowering about driving Athena about in a borrowed or hired carriage—he would essentially be demonstrating how unacceptable his suit would be. He might as well parade about with a sign hung from his neck delineating his inadequate yearly income and the dilapidated state of his home.

"Haven't you any friends who are not puffed up by their own consequence?" Athena interrupted in his moment of self-pity.

"Plenty," Harry assured her.

"Then perhaps you would be so good as to introduce me to *them*," Athena suggested.

"Mr. Jonas Handley will be at the theater this evening, I understand." Harry tried to make the declaration sound like a coincidence he'd only just realized. "He is not, I assure you, arrogant."

"Is he obsessed with trees?" Athena asked dryly.

Harry chuckled. "He is well-spoken and conversant on many topics."

"Perfect." Athena sighed with obvious relief.

Harry smiled more broadly. *Don't count on it, Athena.*

* * *

ATHENA WAS INARGUABLY AWARE OF the fact that Persephone and Adam were not paying a jot of attention to the performance. The back of the box, where they had situated themselves, was decidedly dark, and Persephone and Adam were as near to being *behind* the curtain as possible without actually being out of the box. Athena had seen Adam take Persephone's hand in the moment before the curtain rose on the stage, and whispers, interspersed with the occasional quiet giggle, had continuously drifted forward to where Athena sat.

"I believe your sister is a good influence on Adam," Harry said, leaning over, allowing his whisper to not be overheard.

"*Good* influence?" she whispered back with disbelief. "I swear I have never blushed so much in all my life."

There was enough light for Athena to see that Harry was smiling. "He has done nothing more than hold her hand."

"Then why is she" —a quiet giggle floated around the box— "*giggling* like that?"

"Like *what*?"

"I passed the book room once when they were cuddling." Athena was sure she was blushing all over again. "Persephone was giggling then."

"And you do not think that holding her hand would be enough to make her giggle?"

"Hardly," Athena answered. She had occasionally held a gentleman's hand in the course of a dance. She had even held Harry's hand briefly that afternoon in the drawing room. She couldn't imagine that small amount of contact affecting her the way Harry claimed it was impacting Persephone.

"I assume, then, Mr. Peterbrook didn't hold your hand during your drive," Harry said.

"He didn't even hold my interest."

Harry chuckled quietly. In the dim light of the theater Athena felt Harry's hand slip beneath her own, his fingers wrapping gently around hers. It was unexpected and, truth be told, not entirely appropriate. If he had been anyone other than Harry, whom she considered a very dear friend and, therefore, entirely safe, she would have quite vocally objected.

"What are you doing, Harry?" she asked, even laughing a

little in her surprise.

"I am only holding your hand, Athena," he answered with a tone of indifference she didn't at all trust. He'd used that tone before, usually when he was amused by something but didn't intend to let her in on the joke right away. "It is perfectly harmless. Or so you have claimed."

Athena was about to offer a joking rejoinder but realized Harry's attention had shifted back to the stage. He had not, however, released her hand. She shrugged and shifted her eyes back to the actors plodding through their roles.

A moment passed before Athena realized Harry wasn't merely holding her hand. His thumb was slowly, softly stroking the back of her hand, as if he did so without realizing it. The movement was unexpectedly distracting. Try as she might, Athena found herself struggling to pay attention to the unfolding plot on the stage.

His thumb continued tracing languid circles along her hand, shifting to travel the length of each finger. It was the most peculiar sensation. He was, after all, doing nothing more than holding her hand. Yet he was doing so much more than that. She slid through conflicting reactions. Part of her wished to snatch her hand back; the way his touch was making her pulse speed and her lungs catch was unnerving. But another equally insistent part of her was almost desperate for him to continue doing whatever it was he was doing.

His touch made her skin tingle, even through her gloves. That had never happened before. Her mind continually insisted, "This is Harry." Harry was a surrogate brother. He was her replacement for Evander. Wasn't he? She was keenly aware of the fact that Evander had never made her heart pound in her neck the way it was in that moment.

It was entirely confusing.

The halfhearted applause began, which was customary at the theater from an audience who paid very little attention to the production, signaling the end of the first act. With the tiniest squeeze of her fingers, Harry released Athena's hand. He turned on his chair, his gaze resting on Adam and Persephone behind them.

"Are you pleased that Persephone talked you into joining us this evening?" Harry asked Adam, mischief sparkling in his eyes.

Athena glanced briefly at her sister and brother-in-law and was surprised at the high color displayed on Persephone's cheeks. Surprise was quickly supplanted by alarm. Were her own cheeks equally as pink? She thoroughly hoped not but was not at all confident they were not.

They were joined in the next moment by a gentleman, probably about Harry's and Adam's age. Not quite Harry's height, but with the same light brown hair. There were similarities, though Harry showed to far greater advantage.

"Ah, Handley," Harry said, rising with his usual casual grace. "Wondered if you might stop in for a bit."

"I—" But the gentleman stopped rather abruptly, his eyes wide as they fell on Adam's rigid posture. "Your Grace." He bowed, his voice showing his strained nerves.

"He won't bite, Handley," Harry said, chuckling lightly. "Now, you are already acquainted with the duke and duchess."

"Yes," was the reply, accompanied by another bow. "A little acquainted."

Harry indicated Athena, still seated and holding her breath. This must have been the Mr. Jonas Handley of whom Harry had spoken earlier. He had sounded like the sort of gentleman she was hoping to meet.

"Miss Lancaster," Harry began the usual introduction, "might I introduce to you Mr. Jonas Handley. Handley, this lovely young lady is Miss Lancaster."

Mr. Handley bowed prettily over her fingers. His touch was not nearly as unnerving as Harry's had been. But then, Mr. Handley kept his fingers still, something she was quickly deciding had been the real culprit in the tingling incident. Mr.

Handley's touch was also very brief. Something else Harry's touch had not been.

"Are you enjoying your stay in Town, Miss Lancaster?" Mr. Handley asked, smiling politely.

"Indeed, I am," Athena replied, returning the gesture.

"Has this evening's offering been to your liking?"

"I was wondering precisely the same thing," Harry said, giving Athena a look of barely concealed amusement accompanied by the lifting of that one communicative eyebrow. "More to the point, I have been pondering which part of the evening, thus far, has been your favorite? Or, rather, which part are you likely to find yourself reflecting on later?"

Suddenly, Athena was fighting down another blush. Pulling her dignity around herself, Athena raised her chin a fraction and met Harry's gaze with one of her own. "Nothing about the show has, as of yet, struck me as particularly memorable. Indeed, I daresay I shall look back on this evening and be unable to differentiate it from any other evening I have spent or will spend at the theater."

Harry seemed unaffected. There was no indication that he took her barb at all to heart. "Except, of course, for the fact that this will be remembered as the evening you made Mr. Handley's acquaintance," Harry said.

Athena felt her blush deepen. She had inadvertently insulted her new acquaintance. "I, naturally, was speaking only of the time spent *during* the performance. Those tedious moments will most certainly be almost immediately forgotten. The intermission, however, has already proven enjoyable."

Mr. Handley smiled at that. But Harry, Athena noticed with a secret surge of triumph, simply raised that eyebrow of his once more.

"Tell us, Handley," Harry said abruptly. "How do you feel about trees?"

Chapter 8

ATHENA SMILED AT MR. HANDLEY as she entered the Falstone House drawing room. He had remained in their box at the theater the night before for most of the first intermission, and Athena had found she liked him a great deal more than any of the other gentlemen Harry had introduced to her. He had asked her to ride out with him the next afternoon, and Persephone had granted her permission.

It was a shame, really, that Harry hadn't come across his more agreeable acquaintances first. That Mr. Howard and Mr. Peterbrook had attended the same events as they had certainly could not be laid at Harry's door. If only those gentlemen more like Mr. Handley had made appearances earlier in the Little Season, Athena might have been spared the ordeal of riding out with Mr. Peterbrook as well as the tedium of discussing trees each and every time Mr. Howard crossed her path. Thankfully, neither gentleman was present at the moment.

"I hope I have not kept you waiting," Athena said after the appropriate exchange of a bow and a curtsy.

"Not at all," he replied with a smile.

He had a nice smile, Athena thought to herself. It lacked some of the flash of Mr. Peterbrook's, something for which she was grateful. And it did not have that feeling of barely concealed, contagious laughter that Harry's always contained, but Athena had never met another person, gentleman or lady, whose smiles quite equaled Harry's. He'd even managed to make her smile in those difficult hours after Persephone's wedding. Athena had been heartbroken to part with her sister and worried over the life Persephone had chosen in order to rescue her family from financial ruin. Harry, however, had actually made her laugh at a time when she'd felt like her world was falling apart.

"Did you enjoy the remainder of the performance last evening?" Mr. Handley asked as they began their descent to the ground floor and toward the front door.

"I did," Athena replied, thankful he had not spoken yet of trees nor of his collection of jackets, cravats, or footwear. It seemed she had finally met a gentleman who could be given actual consideration as a potential suitor. He possessed intellect beyond arboreal trivia, was not consumed with thoughts of himself; he was a gentleman, unmarried, and smiled enough to not be dismal company. Mr. Handley appeared to be precisely what she was looking for.

A landau in a very regal shade of deepest green was waiting just at the curb in front of Falstone House, a pair of finely matched chestnuts waiting patiently, a liveried coachman atop his box, a tiger in matching livery holding the horses at a stand. Some would consider a landau somewhat dated for a young, single gentleman—curricles being considered quite the thing amongst that group. Athena was, in all actuality, relieved to see the stately vehicle. Mr. Peterbrook had driven her out in his bright blue curricle, the color chosen to accentuate his eyes, or so he had more than once told her. And he had driven altogether too fast and reckless. His driving had left her fearing for her safety while his conversation had seriously threatened her sanity. This drive, she was certain, would be far better.

A footman appeared to open the door of the landau and lower the steps. Mr. Handley handed her up, and Athena smiled before shifting to sit on the forward-facing bench.

"Mother prefers that seat, Miss Lancaster," Mr. Handley told her, urgency in his voice.

"Mother?" Athena asked in confusion.

He motioned to the seat she was about to assume, and Athena glanced quickly behind her, realizing for the first time that the open carriage was not unoccupied. A woman, swathed in several heavy shawls, and small enough that her head did not come much above the seat in which she was sitting, eyed Athena petulantly.

"Oh." Athena was startled into a rather simpleminded response.

"The rear-facing seat is available, however," Mr. Langley offered.

The rear-facing seat? To offer a young lady the rear-facing seat, when a place was available on the forward-facing seat, was not terribly civil. Mrs. Langley sat precisely in the middle of her bench, not permitting a second occupant to sit there. And, it seemed, Mr. Langley had no intention of rectifying the slight.

Athena settled herself opposite Mrs. Langley, but to one side of the bench, so Mr. Langley would have a place to sit. She managed a smile, reminding herself that older women could be cantankerous. She hadn't been expecting Mr. Langley's mother to be part of their afternoon drive, but such things were not *entirely* unheard of. And it was to his credit that Mr. Langley saw to his mother's comfort, was it not?

Mr. Langley stepped up and, to Athena's surprise, sat next to his mother, she having made room for her son with a swiftness of movement that caught Athena entirely off guard.

"Are you quite comfortable, Mother?" Mr. Langley asked. "Do you wish for another carriage blanket?"

"No, dear." Mrs. Langley patted her son's hand, smiling quite sweetly at him.

He was solicitous of his mother's welfare—Athena could certainly say that of Mr. Langley. Mrs. Langley had the prior claim on her son's attention, not to mention a far greater claim. And they made such a touching picture of maternal affection and filial loyalty.

Athena smiled across the carriage at them just as Mrs. Langley's eyes shifted from her son's face to Athena's. The woman's smile was instantly replaced by a narrow-eyed look of evaluation. Her long, pointed noise and rather piercing dark eyes put Athena firmly in mind of the hunting dogs a neighbor in Shropshire had kept when she was a little girl.

"Who's the gel?" Mrs. Langley asked, her voice nasally and stringent.

"This is Miss Athena Lancaster, Mother," Mr. Langley replied.

"Lancaster?" Mrs. Langley's forehead wrinkled up like a wad of fabric. "Never heard of any Lancasters worth knowing."

Athena was too taken aback to do more than stare mutely.

"Her sister is the Duchess of Kielder," Mr. Langley answered.

"Hmmph." It wasn't a very flattering response. "I suppose she's considered something of a beauty." There was enough doubt in Mrs. Langley's tone to take any hint of a compliment out of her words.

"I—" The single word was all that Mr. Langley managed before his mother's gaze shifted to him. "Er—she does not, of course, hold a candle to your own handsomeness."

Mrs. Langley was suddenly all tender smiles. Another hand pat clearly communicated her approval of her son's evaluation. "I have always been thought to be a handsome woman," she said. "Though I am certain the years have diminished my looks."

"Not at all, Mother."

Another hand pat preceded a look of undisguised triumph shot in Athena's direction. Athena was certain she looked like the greatest simpleton in all the world, sitting as she was with her mouth slightly agape, unable to formulate a thought, let alone a response. Mrs. Langley was as shriveled as a prune. And her wrinkles were not the sort borne of a lifetime of laughter. She had the appearance of one who spent hours on end sucking on lemons.

Mr. Langley continued fussing over his mother as they approached the entrance to Hyde Park, not a glance or word spared for Athena's benefit.

"Do you require many hours in curling papers to create such a riotous amount of curls, Miss Lancaster?" Mrs. Langley asked.

"No," Athena answered, dumbfounded.

"No doubt, your impatience leaves you with flat hair before the end of an evening." Mrs. Langley sniffed.

"My curls are not created with curling papers," Athena answered, realizing she'd been misunderstood. "They are natural."

"Of course they are." The comment was not merely dripping with sarcasm, it was saturated with it. "Your father. Who are his people? What sort of family connections does he have?"

Athena clasped her hands in her lap, doing her best to maintain a calm and civil demeanor. "His grandfather was Lord Henley, though the title now belongs to a somewhat distant cousin of mine."

"That is not a barony of great significance," Mrs. Langley said with another audible sniff.

"The baronies in your family *are,* then, I assume," Athena shot back.

Mrs. Langley's mouth tightened, but she didn't reply. Athena strongly suspected there were no titles, significant or otherwise, in Mrs. Langley's family. Only a moment passed before Mrs. Langley continued her picking. "And what kind of person is your mother?" she asked, her tone indicating she expected to hear something to disapprove of.

Athena gave her a very direct look. She would not endure insults to her beloved, departed mother. So Athena selected a response she knew would close the subject. "The dead kind," she answered, turning her face away, gazing as if mesmerized by the passing view.

The landau slowed to nearly a stop as they converged upon the congestion of Hyde Park. All around them was the noise and commotion of the fashionable hour, but amongst the passengers of the Langley carriage there was only tense silence. Mrs. Langley managed to look both indignant and frail, depending upon which of her fellow travelers she was looking at. Mr. Langley had grown felicitous to the point of being almost frantic. Athena was simply annoyed. From the moment they'd entered the carriage, Mr. Langley had essentially forgotten her existence. If only his mother had as well.

"Now. See there, Jonas," Mrs. Langley said, breaking her blessed silence. "There is Miss Harrington. Now *she* is quite an agreeable young lady. Her uncle is an earl, you know. And her mother is the daughter of a marquess." Mrs. Langley gave Athena a look so pointed Athena half expected to find herself bleeding from someplace vital. "And yet *she* does not put on airs. I do not think we would hear her spouting nonsense about natural curls and family connections that were not worth mentioning."

Athena clasped her fingers more tightly, keeping herself quiet by sheer willpower. If only Adam were in the carriage at that moment. He would set the dragon to the right about!

"Quite right, Mother," Mr. Langley agreed. That was all he'd done from the moment they'd left Falstone House. He'd simpered and fussed and agreed to every bit of nonsense that had dropped out of his mother's mouth.

"Oh, Jonas! See. There is Mr. Windover. Do wave him over. I simply must speak with him."

Harry? Athena shifted in her seat enough to peer in the direction Mrs. Langley was indicating. Sure enough, there was Harry, riding his dappled mare and looking as carefree and unaffected as ever. Harry and his ridiculous friends!

A moment later, Harry was beside the landau. "Mrs. Langley," he offered with a most charming smile. "You are as handsome as ever."

"Flatterer," Mrs. Langley replied with a playful wave of her hand.

"Not at all," Harry grinned. "I have often said that you are a lady whose looks defy comparison."

Harry's eyes slung quickly to Athena, laughter sparkling in their depths. Athena understood then. Harry was speaking absolutely truthfully but phrasing his words in a way that could, if one was inclined to hear them a certain way, be interpreted as flattering. "Miss Lancaster," he said, sounding for all the world as if he had only just noticed her there, even though his mischievous smile told Athena otherwise. "Well met. How are you enjoying Hyde Park this afternoon?"

"The park is much as it was the last time I was here," Athena replied, borrowing Harry's method of careful phrasing.

"Would you say you are enjoying your ride today as much as you did on your previous jaunt?"

"In some ways I would even say this ride has exceeded the experience of my last."

"Oh, I see." Harry kept his tone light and cheerful, but Athena saw empathy in his eyes that nearly undid her determined air of indifference. Mrs. Langley's barbs had not been enjoyable.

"Miss Lancaster is the Duke of Kielder's *ward*, I understand," Mrs. Langley said, commandeering the conversation once more. She'd managed to make the position of "ward" sound as demeaning as "boot boy" or "scullery maid."

"She is, in fact, his sister-in-law," Harry corrected but with such a brilliant smile, Mrs. Langley responded with an almost infatuated smile of her own. Athena couldn't help noting that Mr. Langley knew as much but had not seen that she was given her proper place in his mother's estimation.

"Tell me," Mrs. Langley leaned closer to Harry, her layer upon layer of facial wrinkles piling atop one another as she twisted her face into a conspiratorial look, "do all of His Grace's wards claim to have naturally curly hair as this one does?"

"Miss Lancaster's youngest sister, as well as her brother, share with Miss Lancaster the very great fortune of having been born with the envy-inspiring ringlets you see before you," Harry told her. "Her Grace, the Duchess of Kielder, has perfectly lovely hair, as does another of His Grace's sisters-in-law, though their hair does not curl naturally as Miss Lancaster's does."

"So it *is* natural." Mrs. Langley was obviously not happy to discover as much.

"It is, indeed. Naturally beautiful." Harry smiled at Athena, and something about his expression, coupled with his tone, made her blush.

"It is a shame the gel is so impertinent," Mrs. Langley said, skewering Athena with her beady little eyes. Athena had to clamp her jaw shut to keep from saying something uncivil. "If she weren't generally quiet, she wouldn't be welcomed anywhere, I dare say."

"The Duke of Kielder's sister-in-law will always be welcomed everywhere," Harry countered. His eyes fell on Mr. Langley, pulling that gentleman's gaze away from his mother for the first time in a quarter of an hour. "And all would be advised to remember that His Grace does not take kindly to seeing his loved ones, most especially his wife's family, mistreated or made unhappy."

Athena heard Mr. Langley clear his throat uncomfortably.

"His Grace is particularly disapproving of insults," Harry continued, still watching Mr. Langley closely, a warning obvious in his tone. "Even the royal family dares not slight those His Grace considers under his protection. One would be well-advised not to allow the duke's family members to be made unhappy lest one find oneself in His Grace's black books."

"Point taken, Windover," Mr. Langley said, his voice oddly strangled.

"Well," Harry returned to his jovial manner of addressing them all, "I must not keep this beast standing, I fear he is rather the most impatient of horses."

A moment later, Harry had cantered off. Athena's eyes followed him as he made his way through the throng of people, wishing he had stayed longer, wondering why he had not been at Falstone House that day. She could not remember the last time he hadn't been there before the afternoon had worn on.

"A very good sort of gentleman," Mrs. Langley observed after Harry's departure. "It is a shame his good friend, the duke, has been burdened with such an unwelcome responsibility. He—"

"Mother," Mr. Langley interrupted, sounding more than a touch uneasy, "I do believe we have been out in the weather long enough. Do not you?"

She humphed, though it sounded oddly like agreement. "Learned all I needed to know," she said, giving Athena another one of her scathing visual assessments.

Mr. Langley gave the coachman harried instructions to leave the park at the earliest opportunity.

Not ten minutes later, Athena was deposited on the steps of Falstone House.

"Good riddance," she heard Mrs. Langley's acidic voice declare as the landau pulled away.

"Amen," Athena muttered in response.

Her list had grown by one more attribute. Her ideal husband

would not possess a poison-tongued mother to whom he clung with almost unnatural fervor. She would not spend the rest of her life insulted by a mother-in-law and ignored by a husband who had not yet grown out of the role of needy child.

And Harry, she further decided, desperately needed to expand his circle of acquaintances.

Chapter 9

Harry was painfully aware of the fact that he was walking a razor-thin line when it came to Athena Lancaster. The time he spent in her company was to be the one consolation in all of his efforts to help her to a good match. And yet her company was proving fatal to his self-mastery.

She'd very nearly sent him into a state of panic when she had so innocently declared that holding hands with a gentleman in a darkened box at the theater could not possibly be an affecting experience. There were far too many so-called gentlemen of the *ton* who would take advantage of her naïveté. So, like the dunderhead he too often proved himself to be, Harry had offered a relatively tame demonstration. Those brief moments managed to convince *him* just how affecting a touch of hands could truly be. He was grateful that Persephone and Adam had been sufficiently distracted; a few minutes had been required for Harry to regain control of his countenance.

Portraying an avuncular acquaintance was growing more difficult with each attempt. Harry knew his eyes followed Athena around every ballroom. He was keenly aware of her location at any social function. He had noted her arrival in Hyde Park just that afternoon probably even before she herself was aware of her location. How Peterbrook could have disapproved of Athena's carriage dress the day before was beyond Harry's comprehension. He could scarcely take his eyes off her the entire time he'd been beside the Handleys' carriage today. Athena would be stunning even dressed in rags.

Harry dropped into the lumpy leather armchair in his sitting room. Adam was at Lords. Persephone was probably making morning calls. And Athena, if Harry didn't miss his guess, was most likely spitting mad. He'd seen the flash of annoyance in her eyes as Mrs. Handley had spouted her self-righteous nonsense. He'd known Handley's mother to be something of a bossy dragon, but he hadn't anticipated such a running stream of vitriol. Athena needed to realize that she would be marrying a gentleman's family as well as the man himself. Having a mother-in-law who was selfish to the core and who led her son around by the nose, as it were, would be an unbearable situation. Handley had been the perfect man to demonstrate that. For that reason, Harry had offered to introduce him to the Little Season's fair diamond. But Mrs. Handley had outdone herself.

Harry would give Athena some time to cool off. Perhaps by the time they left for the Fitzpatricks' musicale she would be in a more receptive mood. He sincerely hoped so. There was someone attending the same function who was anticipating an introduction, an experience that was not likely to improve Athena's mood.

Harry slouched down in the well-worn chair, his left elbow on the chair arm, head resting in his palm. He pushed out a long breath, trying to expel the smell of violets that always lingered long after he'd left Athena's side. It didn't help that he'd bought another posy on his way back to his rooms. Harry mentally shook his head at himself. How long had he been so infatuated?

With his eyes still closed, Harry could see her as she had looked the moment she had arrived at Falstone Castle that spring. It had only been spring *technically*. The snow lasted far past winter in Northumberland. Athena had stepped out of the traveling carriage, her cheeks pink from the cold. She had walked up the front steps and through the enormous front doors of the castle with all the dignity and grace that was expected of a young lady of her station in life. But her eyes had given her away, revealing a poignant mixture of apprehension and anticipation.

That was the moment. He realized it looking back. He had seen far too many young society misses who had perfected the art of looking utterly bored with life. Athena was refreshingly different. Constant detachment was expected of the *ton*. Society's upper echelon worked hard at appearing so unimpressed with life as to be on the verge of expiring from it. Harry had never managed the act. And neither, he guessed, had or would Athena. He'd loved her ever since.

Harry opened his eyes. Literally and figuratively. A quick glance around the room brought him back down to earth. To say the room was shabby would have been a generous compliment. Not a single painting adorned the walls. The furniture had most certainly seen better days. His valet was his one and only servant, if one didn't count the maid who came in once a week, and no one in the *ton* would have counted her. Society held itself to a very high standard even in matters of servants. The only thing in the room that couldn't be considered ragged was the violets. And the irony of that realization was not lost on Harry.

He rose and walked slowly to the window, his characteristic smile completely missing. The street below his window was busy, but he only vaguely noted the activity. £650. That was his yearly income. It was possible to support a wife on such an amount, if there were never any children to provide for and if she had no objections to living in a manner not unlike that in which Athena had lived before Adam's fortune had saved them. Except that Harry's situation was worse than the Lancasters' had been. They'd had little by way of money—that much was true. But the family had had a roof over their heads and a home in good repair. Harry's home and the estate upon which it sat were barely livable. Thousands of pounds would be required to bring it to the point where it could be occupied. And even with such a drastic level of investment, there would be no true prosperity.

That he needed Athena's dowry was obvious. But he didn't want her dowry. He wanted Athena. And he could never have her.

Time slipped by as he stood, blindly staring down at the street. His mind was filled with memories of her. He remembered her brave smile the day of Persephone and Adam's wedding. He thought back on the time he'd found her in the book room at Falstone Castle and the palpable relief she'd exuded upon realizing Adam hadn't discovered her there. And his mind relived the discussions and debates they'd had after that on any number of subjects. Harry had retrieved the books she'd wanted from Adam's sanctuary, and they'd talked over the things she'd read. She hadn't summoned the courage to learn to ride, but Harry had secretly intended to talk her into it when he had returned to Falstone Castle after the Season. That wouldn't happen after all. She would be married, and not to him.

A discreet throat clearing pulled Harry from his thoughts. His long-suffering valet was standing in the doorway to Harry's sitting room with a look of urgency on his face. A quick glance at the tiny, dented clock on a heavily scratched end table told Harry he had very little time before he was expected for dinner at Falstone House.

Harry let out a tense breath. It was time to force himself to be happy when he was feeling less happy with each passing moment. He would simply cling to the knowledge that introducing Athena to Sir Hubert Collington would, if all went according to his expectations, add another crucial characteristic to her list of future-spouse qualifications. And this latest characteristic was, indeed, essential.

* * *

Athena sat in Adam's most well-sprung carriage attempting to feel enthusiastic about the evening ahead. She enjoyed music and, until her very long, torturous afternoon, had been looking forward to the Fitzpatrick musicale. Mrs. Handley's company had left Athena drained and out of sorts. A brief nap had done little but make her head hurt.

How was it, she wondered to herself as each jostle brought a fresh ache to her forehead, that sleeping could make one feel *less* rested? It seemed terribly counterintuitive.

Harry handed Persephone down once they stopped in front of the Fitzpatrick house, before turning to offer his hand to Athena, still waiting in the carriage. She attempted a smile, knowing appearances were crucial in the *ton*. No matter how miserable she felt, she must appear content.

Harry's fingers closed around hers. Athena took a fortifying breath. Her headache, though not shattering, was simply unpleasant. And if Mrs. Fitzpatrick's reputation was anything to go by, the evening's entertainment would never dip into the truly atrocious. That would help. Screeching voices and ill-formed chords would quickly catapult her into a debilitating megrim.

"Athena?" Harry infused the single word with an entire inquiry. Her social mask had not, apparently, fooled him.

"I am a little tired this evening," she admitted in hushed tones. "My day was wearying."

He gave her a sympathetic look before stepping to where Persephone waited and offering his arm. Duchesses took precedence over duchess's sisters. Harry would walk Persephone inside and Athena would follow behind. The formality had never bothered her before. But the instant Harry had released her fingers, she missed the contact.

There was something so reassuring about Harry. Even when she was worn down or tired or unhappy, he had a talent for lightening her mind and heart. Her own father had not been one for reassurances and support. He had all too often been lost in his studies, rather oblivious to his children's needs. He'd never been unkind, simply neglectful.

Athena supposed she ought to add that to her list. She would very much prefer a husband who did not forget her existence for weeks on end.

Being in company with a duchess had certain benefits. The other guests parted as they stepped inside the Fitzpatricks' home, allowing Harry to lead Persephone, and Athena in their wake, directly to their seats without the necessity of waiting in a jostling crowd. That would certainly not have done her headache any good.

Harry sat between Persephone and Athena. Around them the remaining guests were beginning to find seats, conversing as they did. Athena took several long, slow breaths, silently pleading with her head to not punish her too harshly as the evening wore on.

"I understand Adam's mother will be in Town for your come-out ball," Harry said quietly, leaning closer to Athena so as to be heard. He smelled musky. Why had she never noticed that before? It was a pleasant, clean sort of smell—not cloying, the way some gentlemen smelled. Mr. Peterbrook came to mind— his scent generally lingered long after he did and was every bit as unwelcome. "She will most likely make a great fuss over you. I thought I would drop a friendly warning in your ear, so you are not caught off guard."

Athena smiled up at Harry, the first genuine smile she had produced all evening. The smile he gave her in return was different from his usual. It was softer somehow. Not that his smiles were ever harsh or unpleasant.

"Windover," a voice said from Athena's other side, pulling her eyes away from Harry's intriguing smile to a gentleman impeccably dressed in a deep green, well-tailored coat, black breeches, and a perfectly executed mathematical about his neck.

Harry rose to make introductions, and Athena automatically followed suit. She endured the usual moment of stomach knotting. She had discovered this strange phenomenon very early on during her first evenings amongst the *ton*. Every time she was introduced to, or about to be introduced to, a gentleman, her insides seemed to momentarily rearrange themselves while her mind echoed the thought that perhaps, just perhaps, the gentleman in question was the illusive gentleman she had been waiting all her life to meet. Despite Harry's expressions of doubt, Athena was still convinced that she would *know* when she had found the man she ought to marry. Perhaps not love at first sight, but love at second or third sight did not seem unreasonable. As she came to know said gentleman better, she would feel it—whatever *it* happened to be. Every time she came face-to-face with the possibility of discovering *it,* she felt a little nervous.

Her mind focused on the introductions Harry was conducting barely in time to register the fact that the gentleman offering his bows was Sir Hubert Collington. Athena did not know anything of him, specifically, but had heard his name in passing. He was a baronet, as was obvious by his title, and Sir Hubert owned a tidy estate somewhere, though she could not recall its location. She also could not recall seeing him amongst any of the clusters of gentlemen who seemed to hover about the fringes of the room at each and every society gathering. Ladies attended balls and soirees and musicales with the obvious intent of enjoying the festivities. The gentlemen always seemed to be present under duress. Adam simply did not come. Athena could not picture him hovering. He would most certainly be scowling and, most likely, vocally denouncing the entire event. It was probably best that he didn't attend, which was presumably the reason Persephone did not press him to join her.

Sir Hubert took the seat on Athena's right side, Harry sitting on her left, just as Mrs. Fitzpatrick ushered the evening's first performer to the pianoforte placed in front of the gathering. Athena rested her hands on her lap, acutely aware of Sir Hubert's presence. He did not smell as nice as Harry, she noted, feeling unaccountably annoyed. And he was not smiling. Sir Hubert wore an expression of undisguised cynical boredom. Such looks were normal amongst the *ton*, but Athena had always preferred individuals who looked at least passingly pleased with life.

The young lady at the pianoforte was executing a fairly skilled rendition of a sonata Athena recognized but could not name. There were no noticeably wrong notes, and the music was not overly loud. Perhaps she would survive the evening after all. No doubt Mrs. Fitzpatrick was saving her best performers for last, which meant if this quite acceptable performance was to be the worst of the evening, there would be nothing truly horrible about the night.

By the time Mrs. Fitzpatrick invited her guests to partake of a very light selection of edibles, Athena had regained a degree of her optimism. Her head still ached somewhat vaguely but did not threaten to undo her.

Sir Hubert sat at the table where Harry had led Athena and Persephone. While she had not exchanged a single word with the gentleman beyond the compulsory comments during their initial introduction, Athena did not find herself anxious to deepen the acquaintance. Perhaps she had simply grown wary of Harry's selection of friends. There was not, thus far, a decent sort of gentleman among them.

"Might I join you as well?" a familiar voice asked.

Athena smiled up at Mr. Dalforth, though it was for Persephone to answer his request. Permission was granted, and Athena found herself in the happy circumstance of having Mr. Dalforth seated beside her. He was perhaps the only gentleman she had met since her arrival in London whose company did not quickly become unwelcome.

So why, she silently asked herself, did Harry seem suddenly very unwelcoming of Mr. Dalforth?

Chapter 10

"How have you enjoyed this evening's spectacle?" Sir Hubert asked Athena, a sardonic twist to both his words and his mouth.

"Spectacle?" Athena repeated, confused at his word choice.

"Certainly a spectacle," he answered with a brief, humorless laugh. "Few, if any, of the performers had any skill to speak of, and even that in remarkably sparse quantities."

"I thought the performances were reasonably good," Athena answered, eyeing Sir Hubert warily. His tone was dismissive, bored, even. But his words were remarkably critical. "These are amateurs, after all."

"If they had been professional performers, Miss Lancaster," he replied with the same mixture of haughtiness and indifference he'd managed with every word he'd spoken to her thus far, "I would be forced to question the future of music in this nation of ours. Indeed, such displays as we have endured tonight would signal the end of refined tastes, were they representative of the very best England has to offer."

Athena was entirely taken aback by his sharp criticisms. A musical evening was meant to be a time of indulgent attentiveness; no one came expecting to be amazed. And, as such things went, that evening's entertainment had been better than most. "I do not believe anyone felt themselves to be displaying that level of talent."

"I do not believe anyone displayed any talent at all," Sir Hubert replied, a harsh twinkle in his eye that indicated he was impressed by his own wit.

"Are you a talented musician, then, Sir Hubert?" Athena asked, searching out the reason for the baronet's disdain.

"One need not possess a given talent in order to recognize its lack in others," was his reply.

"Did you find nothing about this evening enjoyable?" Athena pressed.

"One of the young ladies displaying this evening—"

Displaying was such an odd choice of word. *Performing* would have been more common. *Playing,* even.

"—was passably pretty, I thought, if one was willing to overlook the ridiculous size of her nose."

Athena simply stared. She had watched the performers all night and had thought each lovely in her own way. Not all would be considered beauties, but she had not thought any to be truly unhandsome.

"You must have a very strange definition of 'passably pretty,'" Athena said. The food on her plate was all but forgotten, her shock having pasted her attention to Sir Hubert. The thudding of her headache was sliding around, covering more of her scalp and pulsating into her shoulders.

"You think me too lenient, no doubt," Sir Hubert said, smiling as if they shared some secret agreement. Athena did not at all like the feeling of being in agreement with Sir Hubert on anything. "To me, 'passably pretty' simply means she is unlikely to scare small children or send animals into frightened scurries."

There really was no response to that.

"And you, Miss Lancaster, would be well advised not to stare in quite that manner with your mouth agape as it is. You put one forcibly in mind of an overly ripe fish. If not for that unfortunate resemblance, you could be considered quite one of the more handsome ladies present this evening. At least somewhere in the top dozen or so."

"I beg your pardon?" Athena heard her strangled whisper, her tone the result of her surprise.

"Too lenient, again, I know. It is a failing in myself I work quite hard at overcoming." Sir Hubert sighed as if his attempts at being a complete and utter cad had thoroughly exhausted him.

Athena was speechless, stunned.

"Her Grace could be a rather pretty lady if only her very plain coloring did not render her so entirely unremarkable."

As if to prove that her previous state of surprise was only minimal, Athena felt something akin to shock settle over her. Sir Hubert spoke in absolutely serious tones. It wasn't the arrogant superiority of Mr. Peterbrook. Sir Hubert didn't profess to be, himself, the epitome of good looks. He occupied himself with offering scathing evaluations of any and all around him, regardless of their proximity.

"But, then, Kielder couldn't exactly be picky, could he?" Sir Hubert flicked his gaze momentarily over Persephone, obvious disapproval in his eyes. "Compared to *him*, any lady would seem a beauty."

Persephone didn't so much as flinch, but Athena saw that she had turned alarmingly pale and that she had not completely hidden the pain that lurked in the depths of her eyes. Doubts over her attractiveness was one of Persephone's most tender vulnerabilities. Athena knew as much. Persephone seldom let her poise slip, but Athena was painfully aware that Persephone far too often thought of herself in just the way Sir Hubert had described: "entirely unremarkable." Seeing her sister's hard-won composure had Athena instantly on the verge of tears.

What a horrid, acidic man!

"You are making your fish face again," Sir Hubert said to Athena, nose crinkled as if she *smelled* like a fish rather than simply *looked* like one. "There is not likely to be another gentleman whose desperation allows him to overlook such things. Not all unfortunate females have the luck your sister did."

"You do realize, Sir Hubert," Mr. Dalforth said, reminding Athena of his presence at her side, "these two ladies are the Duke of Kielder's wife and sister-in-law. He is unlikely to take kindly to your slanderous comments."

"They can hardly be slanderous when they are true." Sir Hubert smiled almost pityingly. "No gentleman of discernment could deny that Her Grace is plain by any standards. His Grace, I am certain, has noticed as much. He is, after all, missing an ear, not an eye. It makes sense, does it not, that any lady desperate enough to marry a man like the duke would have to be in possession of a face so lacking in beauty as to have exhausted all hope of making a more agreeable match."

Athena had always thought that ladies who gasped in shock did so purely for the dramatic effect. But the quick, audible breath she took was unintentional and very much the result of her all-consuming surprise.

"And, once again," Sir Hubert motioned in Athena's direction, "Miss Lancaster demonstrates so ably my point about her fishlike tendencies. I swear to you, she looks very much like a carp I caught not long ago at Hoppleforth."

Athena bit on her lip to stop its quivering so she would not give Sir Hubert the satisfaction of seeing that his words injured her. Nor would she disgrace herself in public and give him further reason to berate her. She slipped her gaze to Harry across the table, silently pleading for an escape. She knew that he, somehow, would know precisely what she needed. He always did.

"Your Grace," Harry spoke with all the deference a duchess ought to be afforded but with an air of confidence and authority as well, "I fear this evening's guest list has proven far too *common*," he speared Sir Hubert with a look of such superiority that Athena hardly recognized the usually affable Harry Windover, "for your company. I would suggest we make our way to our next engagement, where those present are more likely to be counted among those on a more even plane with yourself."

As a set-down it was remarkably good. But Sir Hubert seemed unscathed.

"Allow me to offer my escort as well," Mr. Dalforth interjected, the two gentlemen rising to assist Athena and Persephone from their seats.

Harry led the silent group directly to their hostess, and, after thanking Mrs. Fitzpatrick for the music, though he pointedly did not refer to the evening as "enjoyable," he brought them all to the entry hall. The Kielder carriage was summoned whilst the ladies' wraps and the gentlemen's overcoats were returned to them.

"Miss Lancaster," Mr. Dalforth said after handing her into the waiting carriage, "might I request the honor of taking you for a drive tomorrow at the fashionable hour?"

Athena's battered pride was too bruised to prevent a disbelieving reply. "You wish to be seen with a lady who looks like a fish?" she said quietly. The remark she intended to be light came out heavy as lead.

"No," Mr. Dalforth replied, "I wish to be seen about with *you.*"

Athena offered a shaky smile, looking to Persephone for permission. "Of course," was her very quiet response.

"I shall call for you, then, approximately one-quarter 'til the hour."

"Thank you, sir," Athena replied, feeling the sting of tears in her throat once more.

"And, Windover, I hope I might run into you tomorrow as well. Perhaps at our club." There was something in Mr. Dalforth's tone that indicated it was not, in fact, a request.

The tension between the men was palpable enough to penetrate the fog of pain quickly descending over Athena's mind, her headache having built in intensity. She glanced quickly in

Harry's direction and saw him nod minutely, his expression tight. But Athena hadn't the stamina to devote any effort to discerning the exchange between the two gentlemen. She simply wanted to go back to Falstone House and try to forget she had ever met Sir Hubert Collington.

A moment later they were making their way swiftly through the streets of London. The headache Athena had endured on the drive to the Fitzpatricks' was a mere nuisance compared to the monumental pain she was enduring on the drive back. The terms *fish face* and *desperation* echoed in her throbbing skull.

"I certainly hope, Harry, that you do not actually intend to take us to another event this evening," Persephone said, her voice steady but uncharacteristically quiet.

"Not at all," he replied, his usual joviality missing. "We are returning to Falstone House."

Athena released a breath thick with relief and leaned back against the comfortable squabs of the luxurious carriage. She closed her eyes, listening to the pounding of her heart reverberating in her head. Athena was certain that if she could only manage to sleep, her head would feel better. In the light of the morning she might even manage to shake off the sting of Sir Hubert's remarks.

"Come warm yourself by the fire in the book room," Persephone said to Harry once they had arrived, her voice still too subdued for Athena's peace of mind. Sir Hubert's barbs had gone deep.

Harry agreed, managing a smile that didn't look entirely natural. Athena pondered slipping upstairs to the quiet of her bedchamber but immediately thought better of it. Persephone had spent the evening in the company of one acerbic, ill-tempered gentleman. Adam wasn't usually any better. Athena had been unable to defend her sister to Sir Hubert. She would not fail her again.

Setting her shoulders and willing the pulsating agony in her head to not thwart her, Athena followed Persephone and Harry to the book room. Adam was in a chair near the fireplace, an open book in one hand. He looked up as they entered, and Athena pushed down her characteristic trepidation. Adam intimidated her, worried her. But she stood near the door, determined to be there if she was needed.

"You are home early," Adam said, rising to his feet and setting the book on a table nearby. "Were you not enjoying yourself?"

Persephone shrugged as if to dismiss the thought. She opened her mouth to speak, and, to Athena's alarm, Persephone's expression simply crumbled. It was Adam's reaction, however, that surprised her most. She would have expected disapproval— annoyance, perhaps. What she saw was pure, undisguised worry.

Adam was across the room in an instant. "What happened?"

"Oh, Adam!" was Persephone's watery reply.

Adam wrapped Persephone in his arms, his brows knit in confusion. "Persephone?" he asked softly, his tone filled with concern. "Persephone, dear, tell me what's happened."

But Persephone kept her face buried against Adam's chest and didn't answer.

"Harry." There was the authoritative tone Athena expected from Adam. She stepped back without conscious thought and pressed herself against the wall. "Explain this."

"Your duchess and Miss Lancaster have had the dubious honor of making the acquaintance of Sir Hubert Collington," Harry answered.

"And were, no doubt, shocked at the poisonous nature of his company," Adam replied. He still hadn't released Persephone but had begun gently rubbing her back, rocking her slowly, sooth-ingly. Athena found herself mesmerized by the movement, by the tenderness of it. Was this truly the Duke of Kielder? "On whom did he turn his acidic criticisms this time?" There was obvious disapproval in Adam's voice, and Athena liked him all the more for it. Adam could be acidic and critical, but at that moment he was the very picture of husbandly concern.

There was a moment of uneasy silence. Harry didn't answer out loud. He motioned, subtly, with a nod of his head toward Persephone. Athena saw Adam stiffen, saw the look of the Dangerous Duke return to his face. "What did he say?" It was not a request.

"I do not think, Adam, that Persephone needs to hear those things again," Harry replied.

"Again? Sir Hubert said these things *to* her?" Adam's tone would have warned even the densest of beings that he was well on his way to being furious.

"And to Athena," Harry confirmed.

Adam's eyes snapped to where Athena stood near the doorway. She hadn't even realized he'd seen her there. She stiffened, her heart beating faster. Would he blame her? Would he be upset that she hadn't done more to stand up for Persephone?

"Are you all right?" Adam asked. His obvious sincerity broke through her last paper-thin barrier, and she found herself wiping at a tear, a sob caught in her throat.

"Athena." It was Harry's voice, more of a sigh than an actual spoken word. His expression was harder on her composure than Adam's. He looked so terribly guilty, like he blamed himself for the horrific experience of her being quite thoroughly and publicly insulted. And, suddenly, the entire ordeal was overwhelmingly humiliating.

With a sob she couldn't prevent, Athena spun on her heels and fled to the quiet sanctuary of her room.

Chapter 11

Harry would never, as long as he lived, forget the look on Athena's face in the moments before she'd fled from Adam's book room. Sir Hubert's remarks had hurt her. And now, the next day, Harry was still wrestling with a conscience that continually reminded him of his own role in the terrible scene that had played out at the Fitzpatricks' home.

Sir Hubert had earned a reputation over the preceding ten years or so as an overly critical and wholly cruel-hearted individual. But Harry never would have predicted that he would turn his claws on his own dinner partners. He generally consigned himself to commenting on those outside his immediate audience. Harry had further counted on Adam's reputation to keep the inevitable comments directed elsewhere.

He had hoped to demonstrate to Athena the importance of choosing a gentleman with a kind heart. It was a gamble that had gone horribly wrong.

"Windover."

Harry had been dreading this meeting. Charles Dalforth had been obviously unhappy with Harry the night before. And, as Dalforth was privy to Harry's strategy in guiding Athena by providing examples of bad choices in companions, Harry had a reasonably good idea of the nature of Dalforth's gripe.

"Dalforth," Harry acknowledged, dropping into a wingback

chair in a quiet corner of White's, bracing himself for the peal that was about to be rung over his head.

"Sir Hubert Collington?" Dalforth said, his words a mixture of censure and disbelief. "Really?"

Harry just shook his head and quietly sighed. That really had been a catastrophic error in judgment.

"I am assuming he was your choice for demonstrating to Miss Lancaster that she ought not marry a complete jack-a-napes," Dalforth said.

"That was the basic idea," Harry acknowledged.

"Except that unlike Howard and Peterbrook and Handley, Sir Hubert is not what anyone would consider harmless. He is a nasty sort who cares little for the feelings of others. Lud, Windover, the man is not even accepted by the highest sticklers."

"Which is why Miss Lancaster would do well not to consider a gentleman like Sir Hubert." Harry felt practically forced into defending himself despite having been throwing the same condemnations in his own direction only moments earlier.

"And how, pray tell, do you intend to demonstrate to Miss Lancaster that she ought not consider a suit from a man who would beat her?" Dalforth asked, his gaze condemning.

"Are you suggesting I would place Miss Lancaster into the care of a man who would physically harm her?" Harry allowed the affronted tone to remain obvious in his voice.

"You placed her last night into the company of a man who harmed her emotionally," Dalforth shot back. "Gads, man! Did you see the poor girl's face?"

Harry's heart thudded painfully as a vivid picture of Athena's expression of suffering flitted through his memory.

"No young lady should have to be subjected to Sir Hubert." Dalforth looked genuinely angered, and Harry, despite himself, found his respect for the gentleman increasing. "And his treatment of Her Grace was inexcusable."

"Agreed."

"I am not well acquainted with the Duke of Kielder, but if he is not aware of Sir Hubert's behavior, I intend to inform him." It was something of a warning, as if Dalforth wasn't entirely sure Harry had done his duty by the two mistreated ladies.

"He knows," Harry informed Dalforth.

"And is Sir Hubert still among the living?" There was enough serious inquiry in Dalforth's question to tell Harry that he knew Adam's reputation well enough.

"For the time being," Harry replied. Seeing the obvious question in Dalforth's gaze, Harry explained. "Sir Hubert is, I understand, here at White's at this moment. His Grace should be arriving momentarily."

Dalforth's eyes widened. "There is to be a show, then?" he asked with a raise of his eyebrows.

"There is to be an execution," Harry corrected.

Dalforth laughed uneasily. He likely wasn't entirely sure that Harry was exaggerating. *Harry* wasn't entirely sure he was exaggerating. He had known Adam for more than twenty years and had never in the course of those two decades seen Adam as livid as he had been the night before.

After returning from walking Persephone to her rooms, Adam had insisted on the entire story. Persephone had been unable to say much, her emotions too raw and overwhelming. By the time Harry had delineated the insults heaped upon the Duke of Kielder's beloved wife, there was no doubt in Harry's mind that Adam's confrontation with Sir Hubert Collington would be legendary. And, as he was not in a position to defend Athena's honor, Harry was cheering him on.

"Now, if you will excuse me, I was charged with the responsibility of escorting the soon-to-be-departed to meet his fate." Harry rose from his chair.

"Think I'll come along." Dalforth rose as well. "I have

something of an interest in seeing that last night's slights are avenged."

Harry eyed Dalforth warily. "What claim do you have?" Had Dalforth declared himself? Was there an understanding between him and Athena? The idea did not sit well.

"No claim, per se," Dalforth replied carefully. "Merely the interest any true gentleman would take in seeing that a lady is not subjected to public insults and humiliation."

Harry's mind was not entirely set at ease, however. Dalforth's interest seemed to go beyond that. Harry had seen him dance with Athena on more than one occasion. Dalforth sought Athena out at various gatherings. The man was driving her out that very afternoon. Dalforth, obviously, had his own equipage and the income to support such a possession. Harry, on the other hand, was beginning to feel the necessity of tightening his proverbial belt. He generally did not remain in London beyond the beginning of August. He had extended his stay by nearly a month already, and London was not an inexpensive place to live.

Harry scanned the faces of the gentlemen sitting at their ease in the comfort of one of London's exclusive gentlemen's clubs. They would certainly return home with a tale to relay to their wives and daughters before the afternoon was over. But where was the villain in the drama about to unfold?

The room Sir Hubert was eventually found in was relatively crowded. Adam would be happy about that. Of course, the audience would grow once the commotion began.

"Sir Hubert," Harry called out, his voice friendly, if one was not paying enough attention to notice the irony in his tone. "Well met."

Sir Hubert did not look impressed. Harry was not, after all, titled. Such things were of paramount importance to the baronet.

"How was the remainder of the musicale last evening?" Harry asked, as if making casual conversation.

"As offensive to the sensibilities as the first portion," Sir Hubert replied, his usual acidity apparent.

"And was the performance as insulting as the company of one particular person on the guest list?" Harry inquired, keeping his expression innocent and his tone light.

"I do not quite follow you, Windover," Sir Hubert replied.

"Odd." Harry twisted his face in a farcical look of surprise. "I seem to remember finding one person in particular quite odious. Do not you, Dalforth?" He turned to the gentleman beside him.

"Indeed," was the response.

"I have no idea to whom you might refer," Sir Hubert said with a lift of his chin. The gesture was obviously meant to imply that he cared very little for the opinion of two untitled gentlemen.

"Then I suggest you begin thinking, Sir Hubert. Think very hard. And very quickly."

"That sounds like a threat," Sir Hubert replied, his eyes narrowing.

"A warning," Harry corrected. "A warning."

Adam had an impeccable sense of timing. He stepped through the door into the room where Harry, Dalforth, and Sir Hubert were conversing under the watchful eye of at least two dozen attentive gentlemen. An unnatural hush settled over the gathering.

Harry allowed a smile of amusement to slip over his face. "Time's up," he said to Sir Hubert before stepping aside to allow Adam to do his dirty work.

Adam moved slowly, deliberately across the room. Every eye followed his progress. Adam's gaze didn't waver. It sliced through Sir Hubert with an intensity that Harry was certain the baronet found physically painful. Something of Sir Hubert's smugness had slipped away.

Not a breath sounded in the silence. Adam stopped less than two feet from where Sir Hubert sat.

"On your feet, maggot," Adam said without preamble.

The swiftness of Sir Hubert's compliance undermined his grace, making for an awkward rise. "Your—"

"No words," Adam growled. "You have had your say. Now you will listen."

Sir Hubert's eyes flicked briefly to Harry, apparently suddenly realizing the reason for Harry's earlier warning. Harry offered the briefest bow of acknowledgment, little more than an inclination of his head.

The entire room was listening, but Adam didn't speak immediately. Harry understood what he was doing. Making Sir Hubert wait would only increase his anxiety. Eyes were darting around the room as every occupant seemed to search for the elusive answers to the questions, no doubt, on every mind. What had Sir Hubert done to upset the Dangerous Duke of Kielder? And what would be left of the baronet when the duke was finished with him?

In a movement so swift and so expert Harry barely registered it, Adam pulled a sinister sword from the scabbard he wore around his hips and pointed it unwaveringly at Sir Hubert's throat. There was no button on the end. This was not a training session.

"Your cravat is offensive," Adam said, speaking through clenched teeth. With a flick of Adam's wrist, Sir Hubert's cravat fell limply to the floor at his feet, the single piece of linen now cleanly cut in two. "As are your buttons." One by one, jacket buttons fell with a thunk to the floor, the sound echoing in the room. Not a soul spoke or moved. Harry wasn't certain everyone present was even blinking. "And the pattern of your waistcoat."

Sir Hubert paled by multiple degrees as the tip of Adam's épée slowly, languorously sliced his waistcoat into ribbons without so much as snagging a single thread of his shirt underneath.

"But I am most offended"—Adam slid his sword higher, past the point where Sir Hubert's cravat should have been, resting the tip directly against Sir Hubert's Adam's apple—"at the thought of ever hearing your voice again."

"I wouldn't advise swallowing too deeply, Sir Hubert," Harry offered from his position a few paces behind Adam. "There is no button on the end of that sword."

Sir Hubert was nearly devoid of color. He inadvisably opted to explain himself, his words choked to the point of being almost indiscernible. "My words must have been exaggerated by your—"

In an exchange well-known to them both, Harry caught the sword as Adam tossed it and simultaneously wrapped his hand around Sir Hubert's throat.

"You dare presume to utter a lady's name in a setting like this?" Adam's voice was calm to the point of being chilling.

Sir Hubert may have just pushed Adam past bearing. A gentleman did not ever hint at a lady's being the reason for a confrontation or a challenge, let alone mention her specifically. That single breach of etiquette was reason enough to call a man out.

Harry saw the veins in Adam's hand bulge at the same moment Sir Hubert's eyes began to pop. The time had come to intervene.

"If you are going to kill him, Your Grace," Harry said without the slightest hint of concern in his voice, "would you mind doing it quickly? I am looking forward to an evening of dancing, and I would hate to miss the first minuet."

"I prefer to kill vermin slowly and painfully," Adam growled, glaring at Sir Hubert. "There is no satisfaction in disposing of refuse efficiently."

"True." Harry shrugged as if conceding the point. He managed to keep back a smile of deep amusement. They were reaching his favorite part. Adam would offer the offending party a means of escape that was, in reality, more poison ivy than olive branch.

"Listen very closely, Hubert."

When Adam began dropping titles, it was time for the general public to take cover.

"Your presence in London ends before nightfall. And I am sick to death of the sound of your voice. If I hear you have uttered a single word before you are at least one county removed from town, I will personally remove your voice box. You can write out your instructions to your servants. Pantomime, if you must. But not a word. And I assure you, I will know if you choose to go against my edict."

Sir Hubert attempted to nod, but Adam's grip on his throat kept Sir Hubert's head still. It seemed to be sufficient enough agreement for Adam. He unceremoniously dropped Sir Hubert to the floor.

Harry glanced quickly at the crowd as he returned Adam's sword. Sir Hubert was not well-liked. There was, of course, shock on each and every face, but looks of satisfaction lurked in the eyes of the onlookers. Adam would, indeed, learn if Sir Hubert chose to speak before removing himself from the metropolis. Every ear in town would be anxious to report back.

A path instantly appeared as Adam made his way from the room. The look in his eyes was as far from inviting as was humanly possible. Harry walked alongside him, feeling satisfied that the insult Athena had endured from Sir Hubert had been appropriately addressed.

They both climbed into the waiting Kielder carriage and began the familiar trip back to Falstone House. Adam's expression hadn't cleared. The man needed to be pulled from his black mood before he changed his mind and opted to not allow Sir Hubert to flee London.

"It has been a while since we enacted an aborted execution," Harry observed casually. "Sir Hubert should be honored. And my compliments on your swordsmanship, Adam. Excellent piece of artistry."

"I should have shot him," Adam grumbled. Harry knew him well enough to know that Adam was being perfectly serious.

"Probably. But Persephone would have been upset if you had," Harry reminded him. "And she has been upset enough already."

"Athena as well," Adam acknowledged. "I have never seen so much crying in all my life," he grumbled, rolling his eyes.

Harry laughed. "Sure you have. Persephone cried through most of the first few months of your marriage."

"Except she did so in the isolation of her garden," Adam replied, "where it wasn't so torturous."

"If I didn't know better, Adam, I would say you care about your wife," Harry said with feigned shock.

"Someday, Harry, you will meet a lady who wraps you around her finger, and then you won't be so smug."

"Smug? No. Definitely not."

"You're anticipating failure, then?" Adam asked, curiosity in his tone.

"Just bracing for the inevitable."

Adam laughed, something he'd seldom done in the decades before Persephone had come into his life. The problem being, of course, there was nothing remotely humorous about Harry's situation. Perhaps, he thought wistfully, he'd suddenly come into a mountain of money and all his problems would be over.

Harry laughed at the thought. Life never worked out that way.

Chapter 12

ATHENA WAS CERTAIN SHE HAD been poor company during her afternoon drive with Mr. Dalforth. The aching in her head that had tormented her the night before had not subsided with the morning. The ache seemed to have spread. Every joint in her body protested with the slightest movement. Her very muscles seemed determined to prevent her from doing anything more strenuous than sitting perfectly still.

She had apologized more than once to her escort for her apparent inattentiveness. She simply had seemed incapable of following even the simplest of conversations. In the end, Mr. Dalforth had returned her to Falstone House a scant twenty minutes after their departure, expressing his hope that she would rest and, perhaps, feel better for it.

Rest had not come. Athena had taken to her bed, convinced a nap was precisely what she was in need of. But her bones and head and muscles protested every position she attempted to assume. Her discomfort, coupled with a body-wide ache, had kept her turning fitfully and entirely unable to sleep.

She said very little as her maid dressed her for the evening. They would eat dinner en famille followed by the Hartleys' ball. The new duchess was making her debut as a society hostess and it was an event not to be missed. Rumor held that the decorations were the perfect mixture of lavish and tasteful, the supper all that was fine, the musicians superb, and the very cream of society represented—some members of the *ton* who had retired to their country seats after the close of the Season were even returning to Town specifically to attend.

Athena had dreamed of just such an event for years. It would be a ball fit for a fairy tale. Amidst the glimmer of a ball like the one they were promised to, Athena could easily picture herself finally finding that one gentleman for whom she had been searching. She would see him across the ballroom and be unable to look away. Their eyes would meet. She would see the same spark of recognition in his eyes that would be glowing in her own. As if by some unseen force, they would be drawn together, meeting for the first time. He would ask her to dance. And the rest of their lives would simply unfold in marvelous splendor.

She ought to have been ecstatic. But Athena was dreading the evening. She couldn't imagine feeling less like dancing. The very thought of being in a crowded ballroom, conversations ringing in her pounding head, attempting to force her tired, aching body to stand for hours on end left her longing for her bed, even if she couldn't sleep once she was there.

Athena slowly made her way to the drawing room, silently reminding herself of the importance of her societal debut. Adam despised the social whirl. Persephone had managed to convince Adam to give Athena this one shot at making a match. She needed to use every moment to her advantage.

There is not likely to be another gentleman whose desperation allows him to overlook such things. Not all unfortunate females have the luck your sister did. Sir Hubert's words had repeated in her memory until she had every syllable memorized. She did not want to spend her life as the spinster aunt in the Duke of Kielder's household. She wanted a family of her own. She wanted love and belonging. But she had not been lucky thus far. It was her newfound sense of urgency that had her shoulders set and her mind determined as she stepped inside the drawing room. She could endure one evening of discomfort.

Athena stopped only a step inside the threshold. Adam was wearing his dress sword—something he only ever did when he was going out at night. And Persephone was smiling in a way she only ever did when she was anticipating an evening in her husband's company.

Had not Adam said only the morning before that he would "rather pierce each and every one of his fingers with a flaming-hot needle" than make an appearance at an event that would be filled with "maggotty-brained, flea-infested imbeciles"? Why had he changed his mind?

"Ah, Athena," Adam acknowledged. "I believe we are all here now. Time to eat."

Dinner was announced the very next moment. Adam's servants were astonishingly well trained. Persephone and Adam walked arm-in-arm from the room. Harry stepped forward and offered his arm. The now-familiar scent of him was instantly comforting. Athena felt the strangest urge to lay her head on Harry's shoulder, to allow him to stand as her source of consolation once again. He'd buoyed her spirits on more than one occasion. Athena shook off the unexpected impulse and walked in silence toward the dining room.

"Are you feeling all right, Athena?" Harry asked quietly.

Athena nodded without enthusiasm.

"You seem a bit pale," Harry insisted. "And, as I recall, you were not entirely well last evening."

"I was merely tired," Athena reminded him.

"And are you *merely tired* tonight, also?" He seemed to doubt her explanation.

"I believe so," Athena answered. She glanced briefly up at Harry and found his eyes focused on her, as if searching out the reason for her pallor.

"You are certain you are not feeling unwell?" Harry pressed.

"I assure you I am never ill," Athena replied. Growing up in a home where money was in short supply, being ill was a luxury the family could not afford. Daphne had become something of a hand at concocting all manner of home remedies to address minor cases of sickness. She knew which herbs were useful for which ailments and had saved them the fees of an apothecary on more than one occasion. A minor case of aches and lethargy was not significant enough to be more than passingly noticed.

But Harry didn't seem satisfied. Indeed, he spent the remainder of the meal, of which Athena barely partook, watching her closely, his brow knit with what appeared to be concern. He was no less attentive during the short drive to the Hartleys' London residence. Athena found that she rather liked being the object of such pointed consideration. Her father had hardly been aware of her existence.

"Should Sir Hubert be present this evening, promise me, Adam, I will not be forced to endure his company," Persephone said into the silence. The tension in her voice was evidence of her continued distress at Sir Hubert's comments. Athena's eyes settled on Adam, hoping for reassurance.

"Sir Hubert will not be present," Adam said authoritatively.

"I realize he is not of the highest *ton*," Persephone replied, "but he might have received an invitation."

Athena's heart thumped in her chest, and her stomach seemed to twist, only increasing the feeling of burgeoning nausea. Suppose Sir Hubert *was* present? How could she endure it? Adam would see to Persephone, Athena was certain. But there was no one to look out for her.

"Sir Hubert is no longer in London," Adam said.

"He has left Town?" Surprise summoned the words from Athena before she realized she'd spoken out loud. Athena did not make a habit of speaking openly with Adam. He was far too intimidating. "Why would he do that?"

"He didn't, um . . . *say*," Harry answered. Athena was certain she saw a look pass between Harry and Adam, and a twitch tugged at both gentlemen's mouths, indicating they both found Harry's comment amusing. "It seems he was in a very great hurry."

"Did you drive him from London?" Persephone asked, her tone wary.

"He felt compelled to go," Adam replied. The carriage was too dim for Athena to make out his expression with any clarity. But his tone was dismissive, as if it hardly mattered.

"Oh, Adam!" With no more prelude than that, Persephone essentially launched herself at Adam, her arms thrown around his neck.

Athena stared for one lingering moment, too shocked to look away. But a smile slowly spread across her face. It was precisely the sort of scene she had imagined in her dreams. Except, of course, *she* was the deep-in-love bride, and Adam was *not* the groom. To ride in a carriage in the embrace of her husband!

"Her gown will be hopelessly wrinkled," Harry observed, quietly laughing.

"I don't think she minds," Athena answered, still smiling.

Athena closed her eyes, uncharacteristically tired. She had grown accustomed to the late hours of the social whirl over the past few weeks. She'd never been tired *before* an evening began. Athena rubbed at her temples in an attempt to ease her headache. She closed her eyes, feeling every movement of the carriage.

"Athena," Harry's voice was even quieter than before, "you do not look at all well."

The tiniest laugh slipped from Athena. She opened her eyes and managed to smile at Harry. "That is a horrible thing to say to a lady on her way to the most important ball of the Season."

Harry smiled back, and Athena felt better, if only marginally. She was achy and even felt the start of a chill creeping over her.

But Harry's smile warmed her. It always did. And she was enormously grateful for his friendship. He, alone, had sensed her worries at Persephone's wedding. He had sought her out during both her stays at Falstone Castle, befriending her. And he had offered support and guidance during her debut. What would she do without Harry?

"Here we are," Harry announced a few moments later.

Persephone had managed to repair the minor damage her overly enthusiastic display of gratitude had done to her appearance. Adam handed Persephone down from the carriage and pulled her arm through his, keeping his other hand affectionately atop hers where it rested on his coat sleeve. Harry assumed the duty of accompanying Athena.

"There are a lot of people here," Athena sighed, glancing around the entryway of the Duke of Hartley's home. There was hardly an inch to spare amongst the crowd.

"That is generally what is meant by a *crush,* my dear," Harry whispered into her ear. He had called her that once before. Athena knew that many gentlemen used *my dear* rather indiscriminately. Perhaps it was simply habit, though she wasn't certain she'd heard him call anyone else by that particular endearment. "I have no doubt your ball next week will be accounted as much a success as this. Especially as speculation continues to build regarding the prince's likelihood of attending."

Athena smiled. She had seen the satisfaction in Adam's eyes as he and Persephone had discussed the "Royal Dilemma," as they called it.

Remaining on one's feet when every part of one's body protests the needed effort was an accomplishment to be applauded. Except Athena found the polite applause issued by the gathered assembly at the end of each set excruciatingly painful.

Athena walked with Harry back to the seat beside Persephone after enduring a country dance far too rousing for the state of her head. As they approached, a gentleman clad in the black and white that Brummel had made so de rigueur quite smoothly impeded their progress.

"Good evening, Mr. Windover," he greeted Harry.

"Mr. Rigby," Harry returned, both gentlemen offering a correct, if brief, bow.

"Would you be so good, Windover, as to introduce me to your lovely partner?" Mr. Rigby requested.

Athena's usual feeling of fluttery anticipation did not surface, due no doubt to the all-encompassing effort required to simply remain standing and smile with any degree of believability. Rather than wondering if she were about to be introduced to the man of her dreams, Athena simply wished the introduction complete and over with so she might seek refuge in some quieter corner of the ballroom.

"Miss Lancaster, may I present Mr. Rigby of Norfolk. Mr. Rigby, allow me to make known to you Miss Lancaster, sister of Her Grace, the Duchess of Kielder."

Athena curtsied and felt herself wobble ever so slightly, her muscles growing less cooperative as the evening wore on. Despite her earlier words to Harry, Athena was beginning to suspect she was, in fact, becoming ill.

"Might I request the honor of your next available set, Miss Lancaster?" Mr. Rigby asked.

"I had hoped to sit out the next set," Athena admitted. "I fear I am rather fatigued at the moment."

Mr. Rigby smiled good-naturedly. "Then allow me to keep you company, or perhaps I might fetch you a glass of lemonade, or champagne if you prefer."

"I will track down an elusive glass of lemonade," Harry offered. "Miss Lancaster's seat is just over here," he gestured to her seat within a few feet of where they stood, "beside her sister and brother-in-law."

Mr. Rigby paled noticeably at the mention of the Duke of Kielder. Of course, Adam's glare in their general direction couldn't have helped. With a rigidity that any statue would envy, Mr. Rigby took Athena the remaining half-dozen steps to her awaiting chair. Adam performed the introduction to Persephone, though with a noticeable lack of enthusiasm. Odd, that. Neither Harry nor Adam seemed enamored of Mr. Rigby, though they also did not seem *un*fond of him. Athena's mind was far too fogged by pain, fatigue, and the approach of what she suspected was a fever, for her to make sense of any of it.

Mr. Rigby made several stilted attempts at conversation, though his eyes darted with alarming frequency to Adam. Each glance left Mr. Rigby less composed and far paler. And when Mr. Rigby asked Athena for the third time whether she was enjoying her first stay in London, Adam seemed to lose patience.

"If you cannot speak in a manner that at least remotely resembles an intelligent conversation," Adam said, "then stick with standing mutely and save all of our ears the agony of enduring you."

Mr. Rigby audibly cleared his throat, and though Athena was not looking at Adam, she was certain the duke rolled his eyes. For once, she agreed with her irritable brother-in-law. Mr. Rigby was beginning to grate on her already-frayed nerves. Why was it that every gentleman she had been introduced to of late proved remarkable only in the absurdity of his shortcomings? If she was being fair, she acknowledged, not *every* gentleman had proven flawed—only those Harry had introduced to her. She was struck again by the oddness of that realization. Perhaps when she was feeling better it would make more sense, or she would think of a reasonable explanation for what seemed to be an extraordinary number of coincidences.

"It was a pleasure to meet you, Miss Lancaster." Mr. Rigby abruptly dove into the expected exit dialogue. With a bow from the waist, he expressed his hope that they would meet again and, after a nervous glance at Adam, made a very hasty retreat.

"Coward," Adam muttered under his breath.

"After the rumors I have heard this evening regarding your encounter with Sir Hubert," Persephone said, "I am surprised Mr. Rigby had the fortitude to approach our party at all."

"Fortitude?" Adam scoffed. "Idiocy, more like."

They continued conversing, their voices growing quieter as the subject matter veered into topics they alone were interested in. Athena was grateful for the drop in volume. She dabbed with one gloved finger at her forehead, hoping to stop the beads of sweat forming there from trickling down her overheated face. She could no longer concentrate on anything beyond the need to remain upright and not simply lie down on the floor as she was tempted to do. There was no doubt in her mind that she was feverish.

Where is Harry? she wondered, searching the room with her eyes. He would see that she was ill and save her the difficulty of attempting to explain as much to Persephone. Athena felt entirely incapable of any degree of conversation. But Harry would understand. He always did. He sensed her feelings and struggles before anyone else. Indeed, she could not remember a friend who had understood her to the degree he did.

"Your lemonade."

She had not even heard him approach. Much of the ball-room, as a matter of fact, had receded into an unrecognizable blur. Athena looked up in the direction of Harry's voice. "I . . . do not . . . feel well," she managed.

Words garbled all around her, though she could not make sense of any of them. Athena felt an arm wrap securely around her waist as she was assisted to her feet. She knew, on some instinctive level, that it was Harry and felt comforted despite the increasing weight of illness. He would not abandon her. He had listened to her frustrations and struggles from almost the moment they had first met. He had laughed with her, sat beside her when she was lonely.

Athena registered the smell of horses and knew she had been led outside and was being assisted into the carriage. Harry had not left her side, and knowing he would see to her welfare, Athena allowed herself to slip into a dreamless and restless sleep.

Chapter 13

"How is she?" Harry asked the moment he encountered Persephone on the stairs as he made his way toward the Falstone House drawing room.

He had done little but worry about Athena since carrying her up those same stairs the night before. Athena had leaned heavily against him, heat emanating from her as her fever began to rise. Leaving her there so obviously ill had been painful.

Harry had repeatedly told himself that Persephone would take care of her sister. But he couldn't help wishing he had the right to remain beside her, to see to her welfare himself. Harry was left to content himself with depending on the power of sincere and repeated prayers. What Persephone could not do, the heavens most certainly could.

"The fever continues." Persephone sighed. Harry's eyes were riveted to her. It was not what he wanted to hear. "The doctor assures us, however, that she is not in any danger."

"He is certain?" Harry pressed, his fears not alleviated. "He knows what he's about? You didn't consult one of those imbeciles who ripped Adam's face to shreds, did you?"

"Would Adam have permitted any of those men into his house, Harry?" Persephone gave him a look clearly commiserating his lack of intelligence, though softened by the hint of a smile that tugged at her mouth.

"Perhaps he wished to draw and quarter them," Harry suggested with a chuckle. "Although I do believe surgeons are not in season just now."

"No," Persephone smiled back, "insulting baronets are the current prey." Her humor seemed less forced than Harry would have expected, suggesting she was beginning to recover from the insults Sir Hubert had heaped upon her.

"About time you made an appearance, you maw worm." Adam's growl joined the conversation as he approached the landing where Harry and Persephone had paused to continue their conversation.

Adam looked thoroughly annoyed, and he was flinging insulting epithets. If Athena's situation had truly been dire, Adam would not have expended unnecessary effort on either. Adam was extremely focused when circumstances warranted it. Being referred to as an intestinal parasite was, actually, relieving.

"I am assuming those weeds are for Athena," Adam said, pointedly eyeing the bouquet of violets Harry had almost forgotten he was holding.

"Of course," Harry answered. "Ladies always like receiving weeds."

"Well, take them up to her, imbecile," Adam directed. "Convince the girl you haven't dropped off the face of the earth so she'll quit asking for you every five minutes." Adam looked aggravated enough for the statement to be true.

"She's asked for me?" Harry hoped his eagerness wasn't apparent to the others.

"In her more lucid moments," Persephone confirmed. "I confess, I hoped you would come, if only to set her mind at ease so she can rest."

"I can see her, then?" Harry asked.

"Adam and I will be there, so there will be no question of impropriety," Persephone assured him and motioned for him to follow her up another flight of stairs. "You are practically brother and sister, after all," she added over her shoulder.

Harry smiled back but inwardly grimaced. Brother and sister? Was that how Athena saw him as well? That was a rather depressing thought. Sure, he could never be a true suitor or husband. But to be viewed in the light of a sibling! That was all well and good with Jane—who was *actually* his sister—but not with Athena.

He felt unaccountably nervous entering Athena's room. Had she really been asking for him? Why? How ill was she? Was she still feverish? Was she truly out of danger, or was the doctor mistaken?

Athena's bedchamber was filled with bouquets. Word of her illness had, apparently, spread. Harry could identify the sender of each flower arrangement without needing to look at the cards attached. He glanced at each as he walked past.

The overblown arrangement too ornate to be truly tasteful would be from Peterbrook—it was intended to impress with little consideration for the preferences of the recipient.

The small posy that was indistinguishable from every other posy Harry had ever seen would be from Mr. Handley. His good manners would require he send an offering. Handley's mother would insist it be insignificant.

Harry chuckled as he passed a vase filled with small cuttings from several types of native trees. Mr. Howard. Having Adam reject his written request to court Athena had, apparently, not prevented Mr. Howard from continuing the acquaintance. That showed more backbone than Harry would have expected.

The yellow roses were most likely from Their Graces, the Duke and Duchess of Hartley. The duchess's immense adoration of yellow roses was well-known in the *ton*.

Harry paused his progress when he couldn't immediately place the very impressive and tasteful arrangement set on a table near Athena's bed. A closer look revealed the signature on the card. "G. Rigby."

Rigby? Harry had heard Rigby was under the hatches—it had been the reason he'd been reluctant to introduce the man to Athena the night before. He was not at all ready to broach the topic of the unsuitability of men in need of a wealthy wife. So where, Harry silently demanded, had Rigby found the money for orchids and irises and tulips from a hothouse?

Harry glanced disparagingly at the handful of violets he carried. He'd bought them for a penny from the corner flower girl, as always. No wonder Adam had thought they were weeds. The violets were comparatively pitiful, but Harry hadn't the means for expensive flowers. He barely had the means for a respectable appearance and the one or two meals a day he was obligated to provide for himself.

"Harry?"

The voice was so quiet that Harry's heart ached to hear it. He turned toward the bed and let his gaze fall on Athena. She was far too pale, and her eyes were still a bit unfocused, but she was smiling, almost. Trying to keep his expression from betraying the depth of his feelings for Athena, Harry moved to her bedside.

"You see, Adam didn't kill him after all," Persephone said from somewhere behind Harry.

Athena's smile grew ever so slightly. Harry loved to see her smile, even when the effort was so obviously marred by exhaustion and illness.

"He has threatened to do me in countless times," Harry acknowledged, though he addressed Athena, "but," he leaned in slightly, shifting his voice to an exaggerated whisper as if he was sharing a very great secret, "he actually is quite embarrassingly fond of me."

"Idiot," Harry heard Adam grumble. Just as Persephone had indicated, she and Adam were present in the room as propriety demanded.

"You see, he even uses endearments when speaking of me," Harry added with what he was certain was a mischievous grin.

"Give the girl your pathetic bouquet and get this over with," Adam commanded. Harry glanced quickly over his shoulder at Adam sitting in a chair looking thoroughly annoyed. Part of him wanted to believe the "pathetic" descriptor was more a reflection of Adam's mood than of Harry's offering. Though he knew it was hardly impressive, the posy was all he could manage.

"Did you bring me flowers, Harry?" Athena asked. She didn't sound surprised, which was good, nor did she sound displeased, which was even better.

"I brought you a pathetic handful of weeds," Harry corrected with a chuckle. He held the humble flowers up where she could see them, bracing himself for her look of disappointment.

She looked . . . confused. "Those aren't weeds," she said, brow a little furrowed. "They are violets."

"Yes, but Adam did not know that." Again he employed his secret-sharing tone. "And I have found it is best not to point out to the Dastardly Duke when he is wrong about something."

"Even when that Dastardly Duke affectionately calls you an idiot?" Athena answered, her tone teasing but her voice weak and her face growing paler.

"Especially then," Harry answered, trying to keep his expression light despite his concern. He reminded himself that an adoptive brother of sorts would not be more concerned than an actual sister or a brother-in-law. He needed to keep his reactions on equal footing with Adam's and Persephone's.

"I like violets," Athena said, her words a little slow.

"I thought you might," Harry answered, lowering his voice as he watched her lying there, all but disappearing into the pillow beneath her head. She was far too pale. He resisted the urge to smooth the hair away from her face, to touch her cheek, to see for himself if her fever was, indeed, under control.

"I was hoping you would come by," Athena said quietly.

"And why is that?" Did his casual tone sound forced? Harry tried to appear perfectly at ease as he sat in a chair beside her bed.

"Mr. Howard sent me a bouquet," she answered, the slightest twinkle apparent in her tired eyes.

Harry smiled. "I thought I spotted one that had to be from him."

Athena managed a slight smile in return. "He is convinced I think of nothing but trees."

"Mr. Howard does not have the most original mind," Harry acknowledged, but not unkindly. He set Athena's violets on the table beside her bed but found he had to clasp his hands together to keep himself from holding her hand.

"Mr. Dalforth warned me to be wary of the gentlemen you introduce me to," Athena said.

Tension slid instantly through Harry's body, his jaw tight. "Did he?" Harry managed. "And why is that, do you suppose?" Again, his casual tone rang a little untrue to his ears.

"I think he was teasing me," Athena answered. Her eyes were slowly opening and closing, as if the effort required to simply blink was proving too much for her. "Because so many of the gentlemen you have presented have been disasters."

Harry sat silently for a moment. How did he respond to that observation without admitting to more than he wanted her to know? *Yes, as a matter of fact, I have purposefully introduced you to the most ridiculous gentlemen I could think of. I hope you don't mind the fact that I have sabotaged your Season.* Somehow he didn't think she would appreciate that explanation.

"They all sent you flowers, though," Harry finally settled on. "So, not entirely disastrous."

"But none of them knew I liked violets," Athena answered, smiling wearily. "Not even Mr. Dalforth knew that."

Harry managed not to smile smugly. He hadn't seen any flowers from Dalforth. The thought was surprisingly satisfying.

"He didn't even send you any tree branches?" Harry chuckled, feeling his spirits improving.

Athena's smile grew, and Harry couldn't help his own grin. "Or weeds," she added. Her laugh ended in a cough. Without thought Harry took hold of her hand, lightly squeezing her fingers until the coughing subsided. "His roses were good enough, I suppose."

Her continued attempts at humor were reassuring and very endearing. A lady who could laugh despite illness was a woman after his own heart. The moment of sentiment did not last longer than it took his mind to process what Athena had said. Dalforth *had* sent flowers. Roses, in fact.

The yellow roses. They were not, then, from the Duke and Duchess of Hartley, as he had assumed. It was a very impressive bouquet. So, he had been shown up by both Rigby and Dalforth. It was his own fault, really. He would have done better not to bring any flowers than to show up with the raggedy, pathetic handful he'd brought.

There were times when being comparatively poor was humiliating. He'd learned young to laugh it off, to joke instead of showing his embarrassment. "I suppose roses will do in a pinch." Harry shrugged, managing to keep his smile in place. "But the way to any lady's heart is weeds. Nothing else will do." He pulled a single sprig of violets from the small bouquet on the table and, letting go of her hand, placed the violets there instead, gently closing her fingers around the flowers.

"I do like violets," Athena said, raising the sprig slowly to her nose and closing her eyes as she breathed in the aroma. Harry was certain he heard a little sigh of disappointment. "I cannot smell a thing," she whispered with a tiny ironic laugh.

Harry leaned closer, until he was near enough to whisper almost into her ear. "They smell like spring in the midst of winter and like hope when life is bleak."

Athena opened her eyes and looked directly at him. Harry had never known another person with eyes as brilliantly green as hers—even in illness, the color was startling. "I think you like violets as well," she whispered.

"I love violets," Harry answered, his eyes locked with hers. His lungs instantly tightened, his heart beating a touch harder. He had never been so close to her before. Even carrying her up the stairs the night before, there had been more distance. The slightest movement forward would eliminate what little space separated them. And in their current relative positions, they would meet lip to lip.

Not a very brotherly thought.

Harry moved stiffly, forcibly back. He leaned against the back of his chair, creating the maximum distance without actually leaving his seat. Leaving would be necessary, he realized. But doing so in a panic would be far too telling for his comfort.

"Violets are lovely." Athena said the three words so slowly they sounded very much like three separate sentences. Her eyelids slid closed with a heaviness that indicated she was already asleep.

Harry let out a tense breath. He was playing a dangerous game, and he knew it. He struggled more with each encounter to keep his feelings for Athena a secret. Nothing could be gained by giving himself away, but he would lose a great deal if he did. He and Adam had been as close as brothers since childhood, and losing that bond, to any degree, would be painful. He had come to care for Persephone very much the way he cared for his sister. But to be separated from Athena by the awkwardness and discomfort that his unrequited love would inevitably create would be unendurable.

"We should let her rest now."

Harry nearly jumped at the sound of Persephone's voice. He'd forgotten there was an audience.

He nodded his agreement and rose from his chair, casting one last look at Athena. She was still too pale, but she appeared to be resting easily. She would recover, he was certain of it.

"I will see to it that the violets are put in water," Persephone said as Harry approached the doorway.

"They will wilt soon regardless," Harry said.

"You seem very certain of that," Persephone said.

"I have had a lot of experience with violets of late." Harry shrugged. He pasted something of a smile on his face and glanced over at Persephone.

Her look was extremely speculative, as if she was sorting out a very complicated puzzle and someone had only just handed her a very crucial piece.

Harry had never left Falstone House as quickly as he did then.

Chapter 14

"A S IT WILL BE YOUR ball, you will lead out the dancing."
Athena nodded. She understood the conventions, and she knew the Dowager Duchess, Adam's mother, was not only trying to be helpful but was also by far the most knowledgeable person of Athena's acquaintance on matters of society. Athena's come-out ball was a mere two days away. Falstone House was already in a flurry of activity. Adam's mother had arrived only the evening before. And Athena's nerves were on edge. The ball she had been looking forward to felt more burdensome by the minute.

She had been laid up with an uncharacteristic fever for three days and had yet to fully regain her stamina. She had been kept to the quiet confines of Falstone House during her illness and recovery, receiving no visitors but many floral tributes. Mr. Rigby, whom she vaguely recalled meeting at the Duke and Duchess of Hartley's ball, had sent several very large arrangements accompanied by eloquent notes wishing her well. She ought to have been flattered, but mostly she felt indifferent. Perhaps she was merely tired.

"Does the first dance have to be a minuet?" Athena asked. She always felt terribly awkward and clumsy during a minuet. It was such a stately dance, the movements most pleasing when they were graceful and elegant. Athena knew herself to be more suited to country dances, where a little uncertainty was easily masked with enthusiasm. "Perhaps something else would be better."

The Dowager Duchess looked ponderous. She was intimidating—not in the same way Adam was, but intimidating just the same. She was poised, confident, refined. The Dowager Duchess was a very handsome and fashionable woman. And, like her son, there was a sharpness in her gaze that put Athena instantly on her guard, as if every aspect of her character were laid open for evaluation. Yet for all that, Athena could see that the duchess was a very kindhearted lady.

"Adam is particularly adept at the minuet," the duchess said. "And he, as your guardian and sponsor, will dance the first set with you."

Athena had seen Adam perform the minuet. On the few occasions he had stood up with Persephone, it was that dance he had chosen. Adam was well-suited to it. Persephone was as well. They were both naturally graceful, something most people would not immediately surmise about the intimidating Duke of Kielder. Athena was not so blessed.

"The minuet does suit him," Athena conceded.

"But you feel it does not suit you?"

Athena shook her head, unwilling to put into words her lack of grace.

"Let me see you dance the minuet," the Dowager Duchess said, her words not inviting any objection. She rose from her seat in the drawing room and, without prelude, led the way out.

Athena glanced nervously at Persephone. Was she expected to execute the complicated dance right at that moment? With an audience evaluating her abilities? Without even a partner?

"Athena, do ask Adam to join us in the ballroom," the duchess said as they made their way down the hall. "I believe he is in his book room."

"Adam?" Athena asked, hearing the slight tremor in her voice. That was not a message Adam would appreciate receiving.

"If you are to dance with him at your ball, I believe it would be best to practice with *him*. Do you not think so?" It was quite obviously a rhetorical question.

Athena glanced once more at Persephone, unsure of what she ought to do. Disobeying the Dowager Duchess was unthinkable. But instructing the Duke of Kielder to report to the ballroom for a dancing demonstration was tantamount to laying one's head beneath the blade of a guillotine.

Persephone nodded and offered what Athena was sure was supposed to be a reassuring smile, though it did not lessen her unease.

Resigning herself to an early death, Athena turned in the direction of the book room. She knew on an intellectual level that she had nothing to fear, physically, from her brother-in-law, but she was nervous just the same. He could offer set-downs from which one did not recover easily. The Infamous Duke was also in possession of an eyebrow that, when lifted just so, made one instantly begin evaluating one's life, as death felt frighteningly imminent.

Forcing down the urge to turn around and hide in her room, Athena took a deep breath at the door to the book room. She could hear Adam's low rumble of a voice, though she could not make out his precise words. With whom was he speaking? Was he in the midst of estate business? Perhaps he was ensconced with a fellow member of Lords. It wasn't a good time, Athena decided, pointedly ignoring the surge of relief her very quickly reached conclusion afforded her.

But a second voice reached her ears that not only changed her evaluation of the situation but set her far more at ease. Adam was speaking with Harry.

Athena slipped inside the room. Two faces turned in her direction. Athena's eyes darted to Adam, trying to ascertain his reaction, but her gaze stayed with Harry. He was smiling, and that made the entire ordeal easier. Athena smiled back.

Harry raised a single finger and pressed it to his lips. It was a warning to stay quiet, she knew, but Athena didn't understand the reason. Harry waved her over. Athena's curiosity was certainly piqued.

She moved across the room toward the fireplace where Harry was sitting in an armchair, Adam nearby on a sofa facing away from Athena. The air grew warmer as Athena approached, and she was grateful for it. October had turned cold, and her recent illness seemed to have left her more sensitive to drafts.

"Adam has finally been provided with indisputable proof that he is a dead bore," Harry said in a low voice, his eyes twinkling the way they always did when he was in a mischievous mood. He motioned in Adam's direction, and Athena turned, curious.

She could not, even in her most imaginative moments, have anticipated what she saw. Adam sat on the sofa looking almost defiant while, beside him, Daphne was quite soundly asleep, her head resting against Adam's arm.

"It was bound to happen, old man," Harry continued. "The poor girl has endured your company day after day for weeks on end. It's a miracle she didn't expire from boredom long ago."

"Shut up, Harry," Adam grumbled.

Harry laughed but managed to keep the sound quiet enough not to disturb Daphne. Athena simply stared at the unexpected picture before her. Daphne looked quite comfortable, and that state couldn't be entirely attributed to her being asleep. Daphne had to have assumed her current position while she was awake. And, perhaps more startling still, Adam had to have been party to the situation.

"She is here often?" Athena asked, trying to make sense of it all.

"Miss Daphne spends an hour every afternoon with her brother-in-law and, as I know to my detriment, fiercely guards her time with him," Harry answered. "It seems they are quite the closest of friends."

"Harry." Adam's tone was clearly a warning.

"Every afternoon?" Athena couldn't shake off her shock. She broke her gaze and turned her attention to Harry.

Harry nodded, his smile growing. "Although this is, to my knowledge, the first time Daphne has been rendered unconscious."

Athena looked back at Daphne once more. Her dark hair, so like Persephone's, had come loose in chunks as she slept. She was leaning so heavily against Adam that she must have been very deeply asleep. Athena couldn't imagine being so at ease in Adam's company. Had she found herself seated beside the duke, Athena was certain she would have been unable to relax enough to breathe evenly, let alone sleep peacefully.

"Have you come for a nap, too, Athena? Adam, I assure you, has many topics he can discuss at length that should almost instantly put you to sleep."

"You have overstayed your welcome, Harry," Adam said. "Again."

"Throw me out in a minute, will you? I, for one, am dying to hear what Athena has to say."

"*Dying* is a very good word choice," Adam replied.

Athena glanced nervously at Harry. "Is he serious?" she asked under her breath.

"Adam is always serious," Harry answered, but his smile didn't slip in the slightest. "So it would be best if you deliver your message and escape before he makes good on his sadly repetitive threat."

That was not very encouraging. But Adam was watching her with a look of impatient expectation, and Athena knew better than not to obey the Duke of Kielder—even if the command was an unspoken one.

"Your mother has sent me to ask you to join her in the ball-room," Athena said, rushing her words a bit in her desire to have her message delivered as quickly as possible so she might make a quick exit just as Harry had suggested.

"The *ballroom*?" Adam seemed to almost choke on the word. "Why would she wish to see me in that of all rooms?"

"For . . . um," Athena cleared her throat. "For a minuet."

"She wishes me to dance?" Adam looked thunderous, though he didn't move so much as an inch.

Athena backed up and nodded.

"Adam," Harry interrupted, quite suddenly standing beside Athena. "No point shooting the messenger. I am absolutely certain the minuet was not Athena's idea—she does not even care for the minuet."

Athena looked at Harry standing next to her. She had never told him she disliked the minuet. How had he known that?

"If she doesn't like the minuet, then why in bloody—"

"Adam," Harry cut him off.

Daphne stirred slightly beside Adam, no doubt rousing a bit at his raised voice. "Why," Adam continued, voice lowered, "am I dancing it with her at her ball? Certainly not for my own enjoyment."

"Your mother thinks it would be most proper," Athena explained.

Adam muttered something under his breath, though Athena only caught the words *mother* and *torture*.

"What am I to tell the Dowager Duchess?" Athena asked, feeling anxious to leave. Adam's expression was growing less docile by the moment.

"Tell her no," Adam replied simply, picking up a book set on an end table beside the couch where he was sitting.

"But I cannot dance the minuet without a partner," Athena said, her protest feeble and barely audible. She would rather not dance the minuet at all but didn't imagine the Dowager would allow her to back out.

"Adam, you couldn't pretend to be cooperative for the space of a single dance?" Harry asked.

Adam's eyes slung to Harry, his look one of reproach. His tone, when he spoke, was as authoritative as always, but Athena thought he sounded reluctant, as if he was begrudgingly making the admission he offered. "If I move, Daphne will wake up. She has not been feeling well, and I will not rob her of rest when she has been ailing."

The look in Adam's eyes clearly challenged the onlookers to argue with him. He, apparently, didn't realize that his words were far too shocking for something as futile as disagreement. Until that moment Athena would not have believed her irascible brother-in-law had tender feelings for anyone beyond Persephone, and she only *assumed* he had tender feelings for his wife. What an enigma the man was.

"Poor thing," Harry said. "I hadn't realized she was unwell."

"She makes a point of never complaining about anything," Adam replied, a hint of frustration in his tone. "She needs to give herself greater priority."

"Well, then," Harry said. "I will leave Miss Daphne in your surprisingly capable hands and will escort Athena to the ballroom myself."

"And when you are finished there, throw yourself out," Adam instructed, turning his eyes back to the book in his hand.

"Perhaps after dinner," Harry replied.

Adam rolled his eyes but didn't object.

"Now, off to slay the dragon in the ballroom," Harry announced and slipped Athena's arm through his own.

"Did you just call my mother a dragon?" Adam called after them as Harry pulled Athena along.

Harry simply laughed in response.

Walking down the hallway toward the stairs, Athena breathed a sigh of unmitigated relief. Adam made her nervous. And with the unexpected knowledge that he did not at all have that effect on Daphne, Adam was now confusing.

"Do they really spend that much time with one another?" Athena asked, knowing instinctively that Harry would understand precisely what she was attempting to ask.

"Indeed," he answered. "They have an hour set aside every afternoon that belongs exclusively to the two of them. Daphne very nearly skinned me alive when I interrupted once."

"It is a difficult picture to reconcile with my understanding of Adam's character," Athena admitted.

"Which is ironic," Harry replied, laying his hand on Athena's where it rested on his arm. "You see, I found *Daphne's* participation surprising, but not Adam's."

"Why not Adam's?" Athena looked up at Harry, meeting his eyes as he looked down at her. He had a way of looking at her that made her feel warm inside, contented. He could bring a smile to her lips no matter how unhappy or uncertain she felt.

"While he does not allow many to see it, Adam is actually a very kindhearted person. He is hard and, at times, acidic, and he is fearsome when defending his own, but he is far more tender beneath it all than he lets on. And I think he sees something of himself in Daphne. They both, you see, are shy."

"Shy?" Athena didn't believe Adam had a shy bone in all his body.

"Believe me," Harry answered. "Adam far prefers quiet and solitude and does not at all enjoy interacting with those who are not part of his most intimate circle of acquaintances. He has always covered those tendencies by making everyone too afraid to approach him."

They had reached the ballroom. As always, Harry had managed to keep Athena's thoughts off her troubles long enough to allow her to approach the crisis without worrying herself into a dither. What would she do without Harry?

"Where is Adam?" The Dowager Duchess's voice sounded almost before they'd entered the ballroom.

"He is seeing to a rather urgent item of business," Harry answered, squeezing Athena's hand, almost as if he knew she found the Dowager nearly as intimidating as she found Adam. "I have been sent as his less-desirable stand-in."

"Don't say that," Athena replied, struck by the realization that, while he uttered the self-deprecating comment with a smile, there was something like sincerity touching his tone. She lowered her voice, hoping the Dowager wouldn't overhear. "I would far rather dance with you than with him."

There was something strangely brokenhearted in the smile he offered her in response. She didn't take her eyes from his face as he turned to speak to the Dowager.

"What is this I hear, Mother Harriet, about a minuet?" he asked.

"It is to be the opening dance at Athena's ball, and I wished to see her dance it."

"But Athena does not like to dance the minuet," Harry answered.

"It is the most elegant choice," the Dowager countered.

"But, as this ball is in honor of Athena, I think the wisest choice would be the dance that she most enjoys. If she and Adam are both miserable," Harry continued, "you would not be setting a very promising tone for her ball."

"I hadn't thought of that," the Dowager replied. She sounded promisingly reflective.

Athena let her gaze slide between the Dowager and Harry. Had Harry convinced her to change her plans? Was Athena to be spared "ordeal by minuet"?

"What would you suggest instead?" the Dowager asked.

"While Adam generally selects a minuet when he stands up with his wife, I believe he would not object to a quadrille, if Persephone and I made up the remainder of the set," Harry said. Athena felt herself smile—she liked the quadrille. And to have Harry in the set with her would put her mind at ease. "I have seen Athena dance the quadrille, and I do believe she would appear very much to advantage should that be your choice."

"I would agree," Persephone added to the discussion. Athena hadn't even noticed her there.

Athena knew it was the Dowager's opinion that counted most. The minuet would be endurable, but the idea of simply enduring her come-out ball was beyond depressing. Athena had dreamed of a ball of her own since she was very young. She wished it to be magical, to be wonderfully delightful. The quadrille would be a vast improvement.

"The minuet would have been best," the Dowager said.

Athena hoped it was the start of a concession. She held Harry's arm a little more tightly.

"I believe a quadrille would do fine," the Dowager finished. "Persephone and I could certainly rearrange the order of dances."

"We certainly could," Persephone replied.

Athena released the tense breath she'd been all but holding. "Bless you, Harry," she whispered, leaning against his arm a little. He had just rescued a portion of her dreams. Now, if only he could find a wonderful sort of gentleman to introduce her to—one who would sweep her off her feet. But he didn't have a very promising record.

Chapter 15

HARRY KNEW HIS TIME WAS up. Falstone House was filling with the most exalted members of society: the wealthy, the influential, the socially superior, and, to his detriment, the eligible. Not being an actual member of the family, Harry had watched from a distance the constant introductions undertaken in the receiving line. Though he would have liked to, Harry could find no glaring objections to the gentlemen Athena was meeting.

Mr. Rigby was among the attendees. Like the faithful "suitor sorter" that he was, Harry had told Adam of the rumors he'd heard regarding Mr. Rigby's pending financial doom. Adam was investigating, but nothing had been determined yet. So, Rigby was permitted to remain amongst the throng of admirers vying for Athena's attention.

Harry managed to smile at the guests accumulating in vast quantities, all the while resigning himself to polishing his I'm-entirely-happy-about-this face. He would need it during the remainder of the Little Season and would have to fight to hold on to the mask once Athena selected her future husband. Perhaps he ought to consider a tour of the East Indies. Precisely how he would fund such an expedition, Harry couldn't say.

"Any word on the possibility of a royal appearance?" Lord Devereaux asked in an undertone.

Harry smiled, despite the weight settling in his chest. Even the new Viscount Devereaux—only recently out of deepest mourning over the passing of his father—had come to Athena's ball and not, Harry was certain, for dancing nor for the exalted company. Lord Devereaux was gaining the respect of his Peers in Lords, young though he was and newly ascended to his title, but the young viscount was not overly active in society. His wife was never seen. The mysterious lady, it seemed, preferred the country to the absolute exclusion of London.

"The royal response was vague, at best," Harry replied. "Whether or not the prince intends to grace the gathering is, as yet, unknown."

"And whether or not the Infamous Duke will welcome our prince is also, I would imagine, unknown."

"That is the reason for the unprecedented crush you find yourself in the midst of." Harry motioned around the ever-more-crowded ballroom.

"I would imagine His Grace's sister-in-law had something to do with the evening's success." Lord Devereaux's eyes drifted back to the receiving line, only then breaking up to mark the official beginning of the evening's festivities. "She seems to be a lovely young lady, well-mannered and genteel."

"She is," Harry readily agreed; Devereaux was married, after all.

"She strikes me as being a little uncomfortable in such a large gathering," Devereaux added.

"She will find her footing once she has had the opportunity to grow accustomed to Town ways and expectations." Harry watched Athena as she entered the ballroom on Adam's arm. She was most certainly uncomfortable, though the smile she wore would have fooled all but the most observant.

"Let us hope, then," Lord Devereaux said, something like regret mingled with frustration in his tone, "that she is willing to try. Not all ladies will make the effort."

A rather cryptic declaration, Harry thought, especially as it was uttered as Lord Devereaux walked away. It seemed Harry's was not to be the only story that lacked a happy ending.

Out of the corner of his eye, Harry saw Persephone motion minutely. It was time to open the ball and, as the quadrille had been quite universally agreed upon amongst the interested parties, he was being called into service.

Adam was putting on a good show, Harry would give him that. But no one would ever accuse him of enjoying himself. *Poor Athena,* Harry thought. She was so very sensitive and, no doubt, assumed Adam's disgruntled attitude was somehow her fault. Her eyes darted in his direction, and Harry offered a reassuring smile.

"She doesn't appear to be any happier about this than I am," Adam muttered under his breath.

Harry smiled. "She is nervous, Adam," he answered, also sotto voce. "Try not to look so entirely irritated when Daphne has her come-out."

Adam's eyes snapped to Harry, wide for a fraction of a moment, before his usual annoyed expression returned. "I'm placing Daphne in a convent," he declared almost silently.

"She is not Catholic," Harry replied.

"I don't care."

The music began, and thus the dancing, ending the very entertaining conversation. Harry had suspected that Adam had grown fond of Daphne. The fact that Adam had very nearly appeared panicked at the thought of Daphne looking for a husband confirmed the suspicion.

"Smile, my dear," Harry whispered to Athena as the movements of the dance crossed their paths with one another. "You look beautiful and are doing very, very well."

Her smile was equal parts gratitude and nerves. Harry managed to continue with the movements of the dance despite his almost overwhelming desire to pull Athena into his embrace until she looked at ease once more. Her father, Harry understood, had never taken an active role in the lives of his children, and Adam was notoriously aloof and intimidating. If Harry didn't miss his mark, Athena needed reassurance, but there had seldom been anyone to offer it. The fact that she had retained as much optimism and hope as she had was testament to her strength of character.

"Is she going to survive?" Persephone asked as she and Harry met up once more.

"Absolutely," Harry answered. With a kind and considerate husband, Athena would thrive. It was a depressing thought. What he wouldn't give to have been that lucky gentleman.

"Are *you* going to survive?"

But Harry wasn't entirely sure he'd heard the whispered question correctly. Persephone had moved a little too far away for him to be certain. Before he was near enough again to ask her to repeat the perplexing comment, an enormous distraction arrived in the form of the ever-expanding Prince of Wales.

Adam muttered a profanity just vulgar enough to make Harry laugh out loud. The assembled guests would have a show, that was for sure and certain.

At the arrival of the prince and his entourage—noticeably thin of members, due, no doubt, to the uncertainty of Adam's reaction to His Royal Highness's arrival—the music, and thus the dancing, had come to an abrupt and somewhat awkward stop. The guests had parted, as was customary, every pair of eyes darting between Adam and the royal guest.

Adam, looking not in the least overawed, slipped Persephone's arm through his and remained precisely where he was, waiting for the prince to come to him. Harry would have laughed if he'd thought there was any chance Adam *wouldn't* call him out for ruining the moment.

"Is this a good sign or bad?" Athena asked so quietly Harry almost didn't hear her, despite the fact that she was standing directly beside him, or curtsying directly beside him, as it were.

"That depends a great deal on the prince," Harry replied.

The Prince of Wales came to a stop directly in front of Adam. Any other man would have offered a very deferential bow to the prince. Adam simply raised an eyebrow. For a moment the men stood perfectly still, watching one another. The room was so silent Harry was certain he could hear the prince sweating.

Every rule of protocol dictated that Adam offer the first acknowledgment—that he, possessing a lower rank, should bow to his prince. But Adam never bowed to anyone. During royal drawing rooms, Adam would allow an inclination of his head in acknowledgment of the queen and a greeting was spared for her son, but more out of consideration for Her Majesty than out of any sense of duty to the prince.

"This is treasonous, Harry," Athena whispered.

"Adam is more revered than our prince," Harry replied quietly. "This is a battle for precedence."

The prince, Harry knew, was reluctant to concede defeat. His position as Prince of Wales afforded him little, if any, influence in the world, beyond the deference he received at *ton* gatherings. Adam was about to take even that away from His Royal Highness. It was no wonder the entire world was deathly afraid of the Duke of Kielder.

The room had collectively risen from their bows and curtsies, and still the duke and the prince stood watching one another. If Adam's victim had been anyone other than the Prince of Wales, Harry would have intervened. For the victim's sake. Poor Prince George was on his own.

"Kielder." The prince accompanied this acknowledgment with the slightest inclination of his head. An audible gasp echoed around the room. The prince had just, effectively, bowed to a duke—not even a royal duke—and had done so *before* said duke had bowed to him.

Every eye was glued to Adam. How would he respond? Harry could all but hear the question pulsating in every mind.

"Please don't call him out." Athena's nearly silent plea was so desperate and so worried, Harry couldn't help taking her hand in his and squeezing it reassuringly. Her eyes, like everyone else's, were riveted to the scene playing out before them all. "Oh, Harry," she whispered. "This will ruin my ball."

"Nonsense," Harry replied, leaning a little closer, enveloping himself in the scent of violets and soaking up once more the pleasant sensation of simply standing near her. "I assure you, Adam has full control of the situation. He will not allow scandal to touch your ball." *Provided he does* not *decide to call the prince "Georgie" again.*

"Your Highness," Adam acknowledged but didn't so much as lower an eyelid, let alone his head, nor did he offer a bow. The tone with which Adam addressed the prince was not remotely deferential, but more than a touch annoyed. "You have interrupted the opening set."

"My sincere apologies."

More eyes popped at this, yet another example of Adam's higher standing than the royal family. The prince did not, as a rule, apologize for the inconveniences he routinely inflicted.

"As you were not present for the receiving line, perhaps you would pay your respects to the young lady we honor this evening." Adam's request did not remotely resemble a request. The prince obviously didn't take it that way.

"Of course," he answered, his skin a mottled mixture of blotchy red and deathly pale.

Harry sensed Athena's moment of panic even before he felt her hand tremble inside his own. He squeezed her fingers and handed her over to Adam, as he was obligated to. That felt wrong on so many levels. Adam cared for her because she was Persephone's sister, but he knew so little about her, understood so little about her needs and struggles. He, Harry, should have been the one to stand beside her in her worry, to undertake her introductions. Instead, he hung back, melting into the crowd like a good "suitor sorter" whose usefulness had long since run out.

A moment's exchange satisfied conventions and, apparently, drained Adam's store of patience. With a commanding nod of his head and an annoyed wave of one hand, he instructed the orchestra to pick up the next set, and he moved on, leaving the prince to fend for himself. Any other person in the entire kingdom would have been hauled off for treason. But Adam's actions inspired only a look of utter relief on the prince's face.

That look was discussed long after the prince's hasty departure. The only thing Harry heard discussed nearly as much as His Royal Highness bowing to the Duke of Kielder was the unprecedented attention Athena was receiving from none other than Mr. George Rigby, he of the splendidly expensive flowers and supposedly empty coffers.

Harry had been forced to give up his promised supper dance with Athena. The Dowager Duchess had declared that for Athena to go in to supper with Harry, who was, in her opinion, quite like another brother to the "dear girl," would be the wisest course of action and the most likely means of avoiding any undesired talk regarding favored suitors. The irony of that evaluation had stung far more than Harry had let on. Even Mother Harriet did not see him as suitor material.

In the end, it had hardly mattered. When Mr. Rigby had requested a second set with Athena not halfway through the ball, Harry had been called in to cut the presumptuous man out. Having had his dance with Athena, however, he could not be permitted the supper dance as well. That honor had been given to Mr. Charles Dalforth.

An hour after the fact, Harry was still seething. Dalforth was a decent sort of gentleman, and despite knowing that Dalforth had warned Athena against the gentlemen Harry was introducing her to, Harry reluctantly admitted that under different circumstances, he and Dalforth might very well have considered one another friends.

Dalforth, despite aggravating Harry by his very presence at the ball, was not Harry's primary concern as the clock in the front entryway of Falstone House struck one. He was far more concerned about Athena. She had been doing well, apparently more at ease than she had been earlier in the evening. She had danced every dance, smiled genuinely, even laughed now and then. Athena had dealt quite well with the bombardment of attention she had received from an apparently oblivious Mr. Rigby, gently rebuffing him when necessary, repeatedly reminding him that he had received the customary number of dances, sending him for lemonade when his presence was too constant for even the most patient of people.

But Athena was missing.

And so was Mr. Rigby.

Chapter 16

"STAND ASIDE, MR. RIGBY," Athena insisted.

She had been cornered after leaving the ladies' withdrawing room and, essentially, herded into the seldom-used back sitting room. It was far enough from the ballroom to be unnoticed by any other guests. Mr. Rigby's attentions, up to that point, had been little worse than tiresome. A knot was forming in her stomach, however, as she studied the look of unfeeling determination in his eyes. He stood between her and the only exit in the room. Athena knew very little time was required before her absence would be noted. It was her ball, after all.

"Allow me to return, please." Even as she spoke the words, Athena knew they would have no effect. She clamped down a sense of panic, determined to keep herself under control.

Mr. Rigby shook his head, keeping near the doorway, a look of concentration on his face that seemed to indicate he was listening for something.

Athena took several deep breaths. Crumbling would only play into Mr. Rigby's hand. First, she needed to understand his intentions, his reasons. She was certain, however, that he would not respond openly to a direct question. "Is there someone in particular you are attempting to avoid, Mr. Rigby?" she asked, trying to make her tone sound genuinely concerned for him. "I am certain this person could be made to leave the ball." *As could Mr. Rigby.*

He only shook his head, though he swiped at a trickle of sweat making its way down his forehead. His color was not good, Athena noticed. Perhaps the man would pass out, and she could leave him there in a heap on the floor. The idea was promising.

"If you wish not to be found—"

"Not be found?" he interrupted, a humorless chuckle in his voice. "Oh, we are going to be found, Miss Lancaster. It is only a matter of time."

"But if we are found alone, together . . ." Did he not understand the implications?

Quite suddenly she understood. She was to be compromised, forced to marry him to save her reputation. She shook her head, trying to rearrange the dozens of thoughts suddenly swirling inside into something that made sense. His attentions had been pointed—she would not deny that—and yet he could not possibly imagine that she had encouraged his suit. Moreover, they hardly knew one another. Mr. Rigby certainly couldn't imagine himself in love with her.

A dozen discrepancies jumped out at her with alarming clarity. Mr. Rigby was dressed well, but the cuffs of his coat were frayed, the elbows shiny from repeated use. His shirt and cravat were the slightest bit yellowed from frequent laundering. His hair was a little long, as if he hadn't had it cut recently.

Mr. Rigby's interest in her had been sudden and, in retrospect, a little desperate. There was too much evidence of Mr. Rigby's relative poverty to leave any room for doubt. He was in need of money, rather immediately, if Athena didn't miss her mark.

"My dowry," Athena sighed, the pieces falling into place.

"£20,000," Mr. Rigby said. He shook his head in seeming disbelief. "Do you have any idea what £20,000 means to a man only one step ahead of his creditors?"

"You mean to force my hand." Tension gripped Athena's limbs. It was a nightmare. There had to be a way of avoiding that unthinkable outcome. Perhaps if she kept enough of a distance, and if she were fortunate enough to be found by Persephone or Harry, the entire ordeal could be smoothed over. Anyone else would spread the tale with astounding speed. Adam would probably kill them both.

Adam. A sudden surge of hopefulness enveloped Athena. Adam was the key. "You are taking quite a risk, don't you think?" She tried to sound unconcerned, haughty even. "The Duke of Kielder is not a gentleman to be trifled with."

"He is also not one to be made to look a fool," Mr. Rigby replied, his eyes skewering her. "He will not allow his sister-in-law to go about society tainted. He will see that the wedding is held forthwith and all hint of scandal hushed up."

Athena tried to keep her breathing steady. Mr. Rigby had a point. Adam was unlikely to allow her to embarrass him or leave a black mark on the family name.

"But it is obvious that nothing untoward—"

"Hush," Mr. Rigby cut her off, eyes narrowed, though his focus was not on her.

In the sudden silence, Athena heard what must have caught his attention: the sound of voices and footsteps. She stood frozen, uncertain. She did not wish to remain closeted with Mr. Rigby, but being found by the wrong person would be unthinkably ruinous. Her moment of distraction proved disastrous.

Quite suddenly, Athena was held in a vise-tight grip she couldn't escape despite using all her strength. And she was being kissed quite forcefully, painfully even. Her heart raced, anxiety gripping every inch of her. She had to escape! She simply had to free herself.

There was no possibility of slipping from his grasp. He held her too tightly to allow the slightest twist or turn. She kicked at his shins, though her dancing slippers hardly afforded her the impact she required.

In the midst of her bubbling panic, Athena heard the door open. Disaster had struck! There would be no avoiding the outcome Mr. Rigby had predicted.

"I fear we have been found out, my—" Mr. Rigby began in a feigned tone of affection.

In a blur of movement Athena felt Mr. Rigby release her and another pair of smaller, gentler arms wrap around her, the smell of lavender that she would forever associate with Persephone suddenly filling the air.

"There is a reason, Rigby, I am always armed," Adam's voice growled into the tense silence.

Athena's eyes swung toward the sound. Adam had Mr. Rigby pinned to a wall, the blade of his dress sword pressed against Mr. Riby's throat.

"Not the sword again," Harry drawled.

Harry! Athena's eyes immediately turned to him. She leaned against Persephone, feeling her pulse slow and the tension begin to drain from her body. For the moment, she was safe.

"You dispatched the last scoundrel that way and it was, you will recall, a dreadfully slow process, and we do have a ball to be getting back to."

Mr. Rigby paled at Harry's words. But there was something too theatrical in his tone, almost as if he was simply playing a part.

"Persephone?" Athena whispered, as much out of confusion as a need for the continued reassurance that Mr. Rigby was not about to attack her again.

"All is well, Athena," Persephone whispered in reply, her embrace tightening slightly.

"Very well," Adam replied to Harry, his tone annoyed, "you know where my guns are kept."

"Would you prefer a dueler or a hunting rifle?" Harry asked.

Adam seemed to be pondering the question. He was certainly taking his time responding.

"Pers—"

Persephone cut Athena off. "Shh."

"Hunting rifle," Adam replied. His tone was so inherently threatening that Athena shivered to hear it.

"You wouldn't . . . wouldn't shoot your future brother-in-law," Mr. Rigby insisted, his eyes wide with alarm.

"And who might that be?" Adam asked with chilling calm.

"Um." Rigby cleared his throat, eyes darting between all of them in the room. "Miss Lancaster and I were in here alone."

"No. Her Grace has been with Miss Lancaster all evening." Adam kept his sword at Mr. Rigby's throat, almost as if being in just such a position was commonplace for him.

"She was kissed beyond—" Mr. Rigby's shaky voice was immediately silenced, Adam's hand gripping his jaw.

"I despise liars," Adam growled.

"Do not be so gentle with him, Your Grace," Harry joined, his voice noticeably tighter and rough. "I have a feeling Rigby is a habitual liar."

"Habits are easily broken," Adam answered, "when one is dead."

Persephone unexpectedly entered the conversation. "Do be quick about it, Adam. We will wait for you in the ballroom."

Athena felt Persephone pull her toward the closed door. She glanced back over her shoulder toward Harry, afraid of what might actually happen once they left. She didn't care at all for Mr. Rigby, but she did not wish the man dead. Injured, perhaps. But not dead.

Harry smiled at her, though it seemed forced, strained. He nodded, as if telling her to go. Athena nodded back, wishing he would come with her. Harry always made her feel better, and at that moment she needed comfort.

Athena somehow survived the rest of the night. Persephone's unflappable calm combined with the Dowager Duchess's regal command of each and every moment of the remainder of the ball kept Athena from completely falling apart. Mr. Rigby did not return to the ballroom. When Adam and Harry eventually did, they looked as casual as if they had simply stepped outside for a breath of fresh air.

The last guest trickled out at nearly three o'clock. Athena was exhausted. Adam had asked, though Adam's requests never felt like anything short of a directive, that Athena meet with him in his book room once the house was empty of guests. She was not looking forward to the interview.

Athena was almost certain she was not going to be forced to marry Mr. Rigby. That was a relief. But she was not at all sure what Adam's response to the contretemps would be. That he was angry had been obvious. Adam angry was not a sight to inspire confidence.

The book room was blessedly empty when she arrived. Athena had a few moments, at the least, to compose herself. She pressed her fingers against her temples, the headache she had been pointedly ignoring for two hours making itself known.

Her long-anticipated come-out ball had not turned out at all the way she had always dreamed. There had been no dashing gentleman to sweep her off her feet. Her brother-in-law had come disturbingly close to calling out the Prince of Wales. She had been accosted by a fortune hunter and had very nearly been forced into a disastrous marriage. And she was not at all certain Adam and Harry had not killed the bounder.

The night was supposed to have been magical.

"Is that a tear, Athena?"

"Harry!" She was so surprised by his sudden appearance that Athena actually gasped.

He smiled a little, but his gaze was decidedly concerned. "You have had a difficult evening, I daresay."

To her surprise and embarrassment, Athena felt a second tear join the first. She swiped at it and even managed to laugh a little. "It was fairly awful in moments," she admitted, managing to keep herself from entirely falling apart. "I fully expected you and Adam to return to the ball covered in blood."

"Adam is far too adept at dispatching unwanted cads to so much as wrinkle his coat in the undertaking."

"He didn't actually kill him, did he?" Athena asked, not sure she wanted to hear the answer.

"Are you so concerned for Mr. Rigby, then?" Harry stepped closer to her, and Athena felt instantly better.

"I wouldn't want his death to weigh on Adam's conscience," Athena answered.

"Adam's conscience?" Harry laughed. "Are you so sure he has one?"

Athena felt a tiny smile tug at her lips. "Your conscience, then," she corrected. "I *know* you have one. You could never do anything you knew was underhanded or hurtful."

"That, Athena, is probably the nicest thing any person has ever said about me." Harry smiled in a way Athena had never seen him smile. There was no laughter behind it, no worry or concern. It was a look of pure contentment, and seeing it made Athena wish she could bring that expression to his face more often. He had been a source of comfort to her countless times.

"You are a very good man, Harry Windover," Athena said. She wasn't sure where the impulse came from or why she acted so immediately upon it, but Athena leaned her head against his chest, her energy all but spent.

"And you, Athena Lancaster," Harry answered, "are apparently still ill."

It was so like Harry to turn a compliment aimed at himself into a moment of self-deprecating humor. He lightened every situation. She would never have guessed only two hours earlier, while being accosted by Mr. Rigby, that she would have reason to feel so content before the night was over.

"What did happen to Mr. Rigby?" she asked, still leaning against him.

"He left," Harry replied. Athena felt his arms wrap lightly around her, so lightly, in fact, that she barely felt them there.

"On his own?" she pressed, feeling entirely at ease in Harry's arms. Mr. Rigby's embrace had been tortuous. Harry's was heaven.

"Not precisely," Harry said. "He required a great deal of assistance."

"Because he was angry?" Athena wondered out loud. She closed her eyes, trying to push out all the unpleasantness of the evening from her mind.

"Because he was no longer capable of leaving unassisted," Harry answered.

Athena wasn't certain, but she thought she felt Harry kiss the top of her head. His embrace tightened almost imperceptibly. What was it he always smelled like? She recognized the pleasant scent as his own but couldn't identify it.

"Will he spread rumors, do you think?" Athena asked. It was what worried her the most. Mr. Rigby could leave her reputation in shreds or attempt to force her into marriage still. "Suppose he talks about what happened."

"He won't be talking about anything for a while, I assure you," Harry answered. "Adam is nothing if not thorough."

"I shouldn't be happy to hear that someone is suffering," Athena said.

"But you are happy about it," Harry ascertained. "So am I. Adam wouldn't share, unfortunately. I would have liked to have had a go at the man myself."

"You are the very best of friends, Harry," Athena said, feeling the last remnants of tension slip away.

"Yes," he answered. "A good . . . friend."

Harry's words, oddly enough, sounded regretful.

Chapter 17

Harry had been at Falstone House until four o'clock that morning, sitting in on the discussion of Rigby's actions. Adam hadn't told Athena the extent to which he had knocked Rigby around. Beyond Adam's valet and Harry, probably not a single soul knew that Adam had been required to change his shirt and cravat after the confrontation in the back sitting room. He had removed his jacket and waistcoat beforehand, else they, too, would have been blood-spattered. One thing was for sure, however—something Adam assured Athena of—Rigby would keep his mouth shut. There would be no scandal.

Athena had been palpably relieved. For that, Harry was infinitely grateful. But it was not the interview that had kept him awake long after returning to his rooms. He couldn't clear his mind of the sensation of holding Athena in his arms.

She had leaned against *him*. And she had fit perfectly in his embrace. There had been no hesitation, no awkwardness. She had turned to him for answers, for reassurance, and he had been able to offer precisely that. The moment had been perfect and hopeful. For the space of a breath he had imagined himself holding her that way for hours on end, for years yet to come. Then she had called him a *good friend,* and reality had hit like a slap in the face.

Athena had remained in his arms a few moments longer, until the sound of approaching footsteps had necessitated Harry pulling away. He'd taken only a fraction of a second to memorize the feel of her in his arms then resigned himself to being precisely what Athena had declared him to be: a friend.

Twelve hours after leaving Falstone House, Harry had returned and walked into the drawing room, reminding himself he was the adopted brother of the family. It was what he would always be. After Rigby's near-fatal involvement in Athena's Season, Adam was even more vocally opposed to fortune hunters.

Charles Dalforth was there, obviously dressed for an afternoon drive. Dalforth, it seemed, was making a great deal of headway. *He* was not, apparently, to be relegated to the rank of ineligible pseudorelative.

"Dalforth," Harry greeted, knowing he sounded almost as disgruntled as he felt.

"Windover," Dalforth replied. He didn't sound any happier about the encounter than Harry did. His expression was almost accusatory. "I didn't see Rigby toward the end of last night's ball."

"He was obliged to leave," Harry explained curtly.

"His Grace, I assume, noticed Rigby was harassing Miss Lancaster," Dalforth said. Harry nodded silently. "No gentleman should be permitted to make such a nuisance of himself, not to mention the inexcusableness of casting a shadow over her come-out ball."

"As Rigby was dispatched, I fail to understand your accusatory tone," Harry shot back.

"Do you?" Dalforth actually chuckled, the ironic kind of chuckle that had nothing to do with humor. "Who was it that introduced Mr. Rigby to Miss Lancaster?"

"I don't—" Harry thought back, even as he spoke, to the Duke and Duchess of Hartley's ball. Rigby had approached him as he was escorting Athena and had requested an introduction. "Technically," Harry conceded, "I did, but—"

"I hadn't thought you capable of that, Windover," Dalforth cut across him. "I have never approved of your approach to 'helping' Miss Lancaster"—he said *helping* with such a heavy amount of derision that Harry knew Dalforth meant quite the opposite—"but this is inexcusable. What were you attempting to demonstrate *this* time? The desperation of a fortune hunter?"

The remark hit far too close to home.

"I hadn't thought you would choose gentlemen who were entirely objectionable," Dalforth continued, offering Harry no opportunity to defend himself. "Peterbrook. Handley. All the others were at least harmless, if rather ridiculous. But *Rigby*? Everyone knew he was under the hatches to the point of complete disaster. A man in that situation is likely to act out of desperation."

"His Grace will not permit Miss Lancaster to be hurt."

"Which is fortunate, since you seem to have no qualms about it."

"How dare you!" Harry had never been so close to losing his temper.

"I dare because I am worried for her," Dalforth answered, infuriatingly calm. "You have purposefully, knowingly introduced her to gentlemen she could never and would never be happy with."

"I have done this to help her." Harry was angry enough to defend himself even though his conscience hadn't been easy about his approach for some time.

"Help her?" Dalforth shot back. "Tell me, Windover. Did knowing Rigby *help her*?"

There was no safe response to that.

"I am afraid to even ask who you were planning to introduce her to next," Dalforth said, shaking his head and wandering to the windows.

"I hadn't decided," Harry admitted. He hadn't moved since Dalforth had begun his attack, like a man at a mark.

"Was it to be someone worse than Mr. Rigby?"

That single question sent Harry's heart to the pit of his stomach. Dalforth hadn't asked it. The person had spoken it behind the two men. It was Athena. Dalforth's look of surprise told Harry he hadn't realized they'd been overheard either.

Harry took a deep breath and turned around, but he wasn't prepared for the look on her face. Those eyes that had gazed at him so trustingly the night before were looking at him with a mixture of hurt and anger.

"It isn't actually true, is it, Harry?" she asked. "It was coincidence that the gentlemen you introduced me to proved so . . ." She shook her head, her expression growing more pained. "You wouldn't have chosen them on purpose."

"I . . ." But he could think of nothing to say. How could he explain his motivation without admitting to more than he was willing?

Her look grew absolutely stricken, his silence saying what he couldn't. Harry crossed closer to her, but unlike the night before, she stepped back, keeping a distance between them.

"But you were my friend," she said, her tone and expression cutting into him. "I depended on you. I trusted you."

"I never intended . . . It wasn't—"

"Miss Lancaster," Dalforth interrupted. "Do you still wish to drive in the park?"

Athena looked up at Dalforth, the confusion and pain in her face heart-wrenchingly apparent.

"I cannot stay here just now," Athena replied, almost pleaded. "I need . . . I need to . . ."

"You need some time away." Dalforth nodded as if he understood what she was trying to say. "We'll drive through Hyde Park. Slowly."

"Do you promise you won't introduce me to anyone?" Athena said, a strained attempt at humor.

"Not a soul," Dalforth answered with a smile.

Harry's stomach twisted inside. Teasing Athena out of the dismals had always been his role.

"Thank you," Athena said quietly.

She looked up at Harry then, briefly. That look would haunt him, he knew. It was so full of pain, disbelief, frustration.

"Good day, Mr. Windover," Athena said, her tone detached and hollow, her eyes already turned away from him. Then she was gone, escorted out by a gentleman who not only possessed an actual income but who also did not stand guilty, in her eyes, of sabotage.

"I was only trying to help," Harry told the empty room.

The declaration did not appease his conscience. If he were being entirely honest, Harry would be forced to admit that his motives had not been so selfless. Helping Athena find a future husband had not been a task he had wanted to undertake. He had, in fact, wished to help her avoid the undesirable sort of gentleman. The truly helpful approach would have been to introduce her to as many good potential suitors as possible. But he couldn't bring himself to do it.

Being ineligible was hard enough. Somehow it had been easier knowing he would not personally be responsible for introducing Athena to the gentleman she would eventually marry. So he'd spent his time and effort finding men Athena wouldn't care for. She simply hadn't realized that.

I trusted you. Athena's words echoed in his mind accusingly. *You were my friend.*

Suddenly he realized Athena had spoken in the past tense—that she didn't trust him any longer, that he wasn't her friend anymore.

Harry had concocted the whole ridiculous scheme in order to buy himself time—he admitted it—but the plan hadn't worked. Instead of keeping her longer, he'd simply lost her entirely. Friendship was all he'd had any hope of claiming, and he no longer had even that.

Harry crossed the silent room and leaned against the window frame. Dalforth's carriage had already pulled away and was long out of sight. London was always a little sparse in the winter; the trees were bare, society had flocked to the country. Harry had only remained in London for Athena's sake, for *his own* sake. He'd grasped at what little time he had left with her, and it had slipped through his fingers.

"Harry!" Persephone sounded surprised to see him, as if he hadn't spent every single day at Falstone House since arriving in London the previous spring. "I should remind you that this is Daphne's time with Adam. They will both exact rather vicious punishments upon you if you interrupt."

Harry knew he was meant to laugh at the slight exaggeration. He managed a smile as he turned back from the window to face Persephone. "No . . . I . . . ." He needed to get away. Harry realized that in a flash of understanding. He couldn't stay any longer, now knowing Athena was entirely lost to him. "I only came to offer my farewells," he said, forcing the words to sound premeditated instead of off-the-cuff. "I am leaving London."

"This is unexpected," Persephone replied, moving closer to him, her eyes searching his face. "I hope there is nothing wrong, that there isn't trouble at your estate."

Harry smiled and even laughed lightly. "There is always trouble at my estate," he replied. "But as there is little I can do about it, I am seldom informed of the newest disastrous developments."

Persephone's look was so full of commiseration that Harry found himself actually smiling genuinely, if not broadly. Persephone well understood the difficulties of financial hardship.

"Actually, I am"—he thought frantically—"going to visit my sister. I have not seen Jane since coming to Town."

Jane, Harry's older sister and his only sibling, lived in Lincolnshire, far enough from London to negate the possibility of a day trip up to see her when he was in Town and far enough from Falstone Castle, where Harry spent the rest of the year, to make visits further between than they ought to be. Jane and her husband would take Harry in for a while, until he decided how to go forward. Falstone Castle would not be the welcome abode it had once been.

"Will you be returning to London?" Persephone asked.

"No," Harry answered. *Not a chance.* "The Little Season is very nearly at an end."

"True." So why did Persephone sound unconvinced by his explanation. "And shall we expect you at Christmas?"

Harry closed his eyes against the memory of the last Christmas he had spent at Falstone Castle. Athena had been there. He'd first realized then that he was growing rather infatuated with her. He hadn't been top-over-tail in love with her yet, but it had been, by far, the most pleasant holiday he'd spent since before his parents had died. Adam and Persephone had finally found happiness with one another. The youngest Lancaster sister had added the joy only children can bring to a celebration. And Athena had repeatedly taken Harry's breath away, with both her beauty and her charm, though she seemed entirely unaware that she possessed either one.

"I don't know that I will make it to Falstone Castle for Christmas this year," Harry said, his heart sinking as he voiced the bleak future ahead of him. His days at Falstone had ended for all intents and purposes. He couldn't bear to be there, despised by the lady he loved, or watching her finding her own happiness with someone other than himself.

"You know that you are always welcome," Persephone insisted, concern creasing her forehead.

Harry smiled tightly and nodded. "I will be leaving forthwith, so I really should be on my way back to my rooms to pack."

"Have you any message for Adam?" Persephone looked very much like she was studying him closely, searching for what he wasn't saying. Why had Harry never realized how piercing her gaze could be?

"Just tell him I took myself off," Harry answered, striving for his usual jovial tone. "He'll say, 'It's about time.'"

"And then act very satisfied with himself," Persephone added with a light laugh. "And for Athena? Have you no parting words for her?"

I am sorry. I never meant to cause you pain. Please forgive me. I love you. "No."

* * *

Harry was crammed into the uncomfortable corner of a traveling coach before dinnertime. Not one of his fellow passengers smiled or greeted him. But, then, he had neither smiled nor greeted them. He found he had no desire to make conversation and no reason to smile.

Chapter 18

"IF HE WERE STILL IN London, I'd kill him," Adam grumbled. He'd uttered myriad variations on that threat over the week since Harry had left London.

There were moments when Athena wholeheartedly agreed. Those moments, however, were invariably followed by the realization that she missed Harry almost desperately despite the fact that she was hurt and angry with him. Mr. Howard had launched into one of his rambling discourses on trees of northern England only the evening before at a soiree. Athena had, out of habit, turned to smile at Harry, but he hadn't been beside her as he'd once always been. A moment before she'd been entirely downtrodden with wishing Harry hadn't left, Athena had reminded herself that Harry had introduced her to Mr. Howard in the first place.

"Harry is certainly entitled to visit his sister, Adam," Persephone said.

"He has a ridiculous sense of timing," Adam said, his eyes turned to the dark street outside their moving carriage. "A few more weeks and this abysmal Little Season will be over with. The man couldn't have waited that long?"

"He probably wanted to make the journey before the roads up north are all but impassable," Persephone pointed out.

"We are going to have to leave in a fortnight or so as it is," Adam agreed, "or we'll never make it to Falstone Castle."

"Can you endure another two weeks of society?" Persephone asked, an obvious smile in her tone, though the carriage interior was too dark for Athena to see her clearly.

"Barely." He sounded like he was holding back a laugh.

The rest of the ride was silent. It was not the most promising beginning to the night's festivities. Adam tolerated the theater more than any other activity, probably owing to the fact that there was little, if any, need to interact with anyone beyond his own group. Persephone had begun to look a bit pulled over the past week, no doubt the constant activity of the months she'd spent in London having worn her to a thread.

Athena, for her part, felt mostly anxious. She had known the Little Season was nearly at a close. Until Adam had declared they would remain in London for not more than another fortnight, she had been planning on another month. How could she possibly fall in love in two weeks?

In her mind, it had all seemed so simple. The gentleman of her dreams would find her, and she would know he was exactly the companion she had been waiting for. She spent most of the opening act of whichever performance they were watching reflecting on her expectations. The scenario had replayed in her mind so many times over the course of her life that she had it memorized. But every ball came and went without the heart-pounding moment of seeing her heart's desire across the ballroom, without watching him slowly make his way to where she stood, without the tingling touch of hands.

She was running out of time. Adam would not wish to spend another Season sponsoring her, and she had no wish to be alone all her life. Without Harry to help her . . . But Athena didn't allow the thought to continue. Harry, apparently, had *not* helped her.

"You appear to be rather deep in thought." Mr. Dalforth's voice snapped Athena from her state of reflection. Around her, the audience was loudly conversing—even more loudly than they generally did *during* the performance—indicating that Athena's inattention had been so complete she had not even noticed the start of the first intermission.

"I suppose I was wool gathering," Athena acknowledged, trying to keep her tone light.

"You have seemed a bit distracted the last few days." His words were hesitant and his look a little wary, almost as if he was unsure he wanted to hear her reasons.

Had Harry been asking, Athena would have told him everything. Confiding in Harry came easily, naturally. There was never any worry of censure or dismissal from him. Not that Mr. Dalforth was ever unkind. He simply didn't inspire the same level of trust that Harry did, or *had*. She was so confused. Trust had always been the feeling she'd associated most with Harry, and he had betrayed her, had deceived her for weeks. But—drat the man—despite it all, she wished he was there.

"The general consensus seems to be that it will snow by morning," Mr. Dalforth said as if he were continuing some previous thread of conversation. Athena realized she hadn't really been listening and devoted herself to paying closer attention. "So perhaps tea would be the better option after all."

Her confusion must have shown. Mr. Dalforth smiled at her, perhaps a little chagrined. "As the weather is likely to be unco-operative tomorrow, I was suggesting we forgo our scheduled ride in the park and remain at Falstone House to take tea with your sister, should she agree."

"That is probably wise," Athena acknowledged.

Mr. Dalforth had driven her out thrice since Harry had left London and a handful of times before then. He danced with her at each ball, though never more than once. As he was at that moment, Mr. Dalforth was also certain to pay his respects whenever they were in attendance at the same function. "Pointed" she had overheard a dowager refer to the attention Athena was receiving from Mr. Dalforth. "Promising" was another descriptor used.

Based on the evaluation of curious onlookers, there was a very real possibility that Mr. Dalforth was courting her. Indeed, the more she thought on it, the more certain Athena became. Shouldn't a young lady who is being courted realize as much? It certainly ought not to come as an epiphanic insight several weeks after the fact.

Athena looked more closely at Mr. Dalforth as he consulted Persephone on the change of plans for the next afternoon. Somehow she had imagined a far more noticeable reaction to a gentleman who was courting her. She had fully believed that her heart would warm at the sight of her would-be suitor, that she would be inexplicably pleased to have him nearby, would perhaps even feel a flip of her heart upon seeing him after even a short separation. She hadn't even noticed when he'd come into their box. And, at the moment, she had absolutely no idea what he was saying.

Athena paid more attention the rest of the evening. Mr. Dalforth remained in their box until the second intermission. Her heart did not misbehave, and she found she was not overly disappointed when he took his leave. Mr. Dalforth was a very kind, intelligent, and conversant gentleman. He was not ridiculously conceited nor did he possess a dragon of a mother. He had all the qualities she had already decided she desired in a future husband, including those she had added after Harry's eventually disastrous involvement in her Little Season.

But it did not feel like enough. There was no spark, no rush of emotion between them. A gentleman did not pay a lady so much obvious and public attention as she had been receiving from Mr. Dalforth unless he was either a relative or intending to marry her. When she had made her bows to society, Athena had hoped she would receive an offer before her Season was over. That outcome suddenly seemed imminent. But rather than feeling relieved or excited or happy, Athena felt very nearly panicked.

* * *

"Hiding in the rhododendrons, Harry?" Jane was laughing, probably *at* him.

Harry looked up from his seat on a bench in the garden and smiled at his sister. She had the same blue eyes he did, eyes that, at that moment, appeared to be full of amusement. "I was hoping to avoid my gossip-loving sister," Harry answered, shifting his look into one of feigned worry. "I have feared for my constitution from the moment I arrived, knowing she would harangue me for all the latest *on dits* and that the undertaking would require several hours at the least. I am not certain I have the stamina." Harry managed an exaggerated sigh.

"*That* sister will catch up with you eventually," Jane replied.

"And which sister has cornered me just now?" Harry asked, laughing a little.

"The one who is wondering what brought her usually cheerful brother up from Town when the Duke of Kielder is still in London," Jane answered. "That has not happened since Claudius was born."

"Well, the *rest* of your children had the decency to make their debut when I was at Falstone Castle," Harry answered. "Perhaps I came in anticipation of *this* one," Harry motioned slightly with his head toward the very obvious roundness of his sister's figure.

Jane shook her head, still smiling in amusement. "You know very well this child will not arrive until the new year. No, it is not that which has brought you to Lincolnshire." She looked at him speculatively. Harry attempted to look entirely at his ease. "Has His Grace finally decided to do away with you?"

Harry had to laugh, just as Jane did. She had been frightened beyond bearing when she'd first met Adam. He had been ten years old at the time. Jane had been twelve. Adam had already gained a reputation for being fearsome, and he had long since perfected his ducal air. Adam had spent the Christmas holiday with Harry's aunt and uncle in Scotland. By the end of the visit, Jane was referring to Adam—though not in his presence—as a "tortured soul," and while she was certainly not *un*intimidated by him, she had decided Adam was not on the verge of murdering her brother. After a few more years passed without word of Harry's untimely death, Jane became less concerned, even joking about the potential for a violent end to Harry and Adam's unexpected friendship.

"Did you . . ." Jane looked a little uncomfortable but, being the unsympathetic sister she often was, pressed on regardless. "Did you run out of money? You were in Town longer than usual, and I know how expensive London can be."

"No," Harry reassured her, squeezing her hand where it rested on the bench. Jane knew better than anyone, except perhaps for Adam, how dire Harry's circumstances really were. If Jane's husband hadn't fallen top-over-tail in love with Harry's sometimes-flighty sister after a nearly disastrous courtship the summer Jane had spent in Bath as a hired companion, Jane would yet be fetching wraps and tea for some curmudgeonly old lady or another. The estate could not support one gentleman, let alone a lady in addition. "I was particularly careful." He knew Jane needed to have her mind set at ease on that score. She often expressed a wish to help, an impossible thing, considering the ever-increasing size of their family coupled with her husband's modest income contrasted against the enormity of the Windover estate's needs. "And Adam saw to it that I ate regularly."

"You know, for an ogre, he is remarkably thoughtful," Jane replied, the twinkle in her eyes evident once again.

"Yes, he is a very well-mannered monster."

"So if the Dastardly Duke didn't drive you from London and your creditors aren't up in arms, that leaves only one possibility." Jane shrugged dramatically.

"And what is that?" Harry asked with a grin.

She lowered her voice to a whisper, her eyes growing wide. Jane was nothing if not theatrical. "You have run afoul of the most viciously vengeful of all the gods."

Harry matched her dramatic whisper. "Is that not a rather pagan thing to say within throwing distance of a church?"

"It is not throwing distance if one is throwing something heavy enough," she answered.

"Ah. Proceed."

They had ever been like that, playing off each other and going to great lengths to try to get the other to laugh.

"I don't remember what I was saying," Jane answered in her unwaveringly serious whisper.

"The god I have offended," Harry hinted.

"Ah, yes. The god of—" She looked around, darting her eyes as if searching for an enemy army about to descend upon them. "Love."

"You believe a lady has driven me from London?" Harry managed to smile as if it were humorous.

"Ah!" It was a look of epiphany if Harry had ever seen one. "I believe I have hit upon it."

Jane knew him too well. Harry sighed and shook his head in defeat, though with a smile. One couldn't help smiling with Jane. Athena had the same effect on him, though Harry appreciated that she had a more serious side. He often wondered how Jane's husband put up with her constant teasing and joking. Harry was not so lacking in self-awareness not to realize he was a great deal like his sister. He also understood that he would never endure being married to someone precisely like himself.

"What is the lady's name?" Jane asked, far too much excitement in her voice.

"Apparently you believe I left my wits in London as well as my heart." Harry chuckled. He would *never* tell his sister the source of his heartache. She would most likely do something entirely disastrous, like write to Athena directly. Jane was enthusiastic but did not always think things through very well.

"You don't wish to tell me?" Jane asked. "Why ever not? She's not married is she?"

"Of course she's not married." Harry rolled his eyes.

"Thank the heavens!" But Jane's tone was so exaggerated that Harry did not take her seriously for one moment. "For then I would have been forced to preach to you—we are within throwing distance of a church, after all—and I do not enjoy moralizing to my brother."

Harry laughed again. "So now that the subject of my moral fortitude has been put to rest, might we move on?"

"Oh, but we have not at all settled the issue of your bleeding heart."

"Very dramatically put, sister," Harry said.

"Thank you." She offered something of a curtsy, which was impressive considering she was both sitting and largely expectant. "Was the lady not interested then? Or ineligible?"

"I do not know that she was interested," Harry answered, the admission painful. "It hardly mattered, however, as *I* was considered extremely ineligible."

"Ineligible how?" Jane demanded. She ever had been extremely protective of Harry, much like a mother hen with her chick.

"Her guardian is quite specifically opposed to fortune hunters," Harry admitted.

"You would never marry someone simply for her dowry," Jane defended.

"But the fact remains, Jane, that I have a dilapidated estate and almost no income. And she—"

"No doubt, has an enormous dowry," Jane finished for him.

"Almost vulgarly enormous," Harry conceded. "The discrepancy alone labels me a fortune hunter."

"And so you simply gave up?" It was something of a scold. Harry couldn't blame her for thinking so. She was not aware of how long he'd held on to such a hopeless wish.

Harry looked away from his sister, his eyes sliding over the garden, though not seeing anything in particular. "I could not bear it any longer," he said.

Jane was silent beside him. After a moment she spoke, her tone soft and gentle. "You care a great deal for her, I daresay."

"I cannot imagine ever loving anyone else." It was nothing but the truth, though he'd never spoken his feelings out loud before.

"Oh, Harry." He felt Jane squeeze his hand.

The discussion had grown too serious for Harry's taste. He had left London to escape heaviness and depression. "So I have come here to be pummeled by your unscrupulous offspring."

"I am certain they will oblige you with fervor," Jane replied, obviously catching on to the hint in his forced-jovial tone. "I could even provide them with sticks and such."

"Weaponry will be unnecessary."

He helped her to her feet, and they walked back toward the house in silence. Being with Jane's family would help, to a degree. With four young children, there would be ample distraction. But seeing her loving and growing family would only serve as a reminder of what Harry would never have. And he had discovered nearly a year earlier that nothing ever entirely pushed thoughts of Athena from his mind.

Chapter 19

ADAM HAD QUITE ADAMANTLY REFUSED to join Persephone and Athena for tea, despite knowing Mr. Dalforth was expected. His visit had been discussed that morning over breakfast.

"Suppose Mr. Dalforth wishes to speak with you," Persephone had said rather urgently.

"Then you can give him directions," Adam had replied. "I will be in my book room. I have absolutely no intention of altering my schedule for something as mundane as an afternoon tea."

Athena had instantly stiffened. Adam disliked everything that was essential to her having a Season. She could not expect him to endure a second round. She would simply have to accept any offer that was forthcoming if she wished to make a match.

"Mundane?" Persephone had replied. "And suppose Mr. Dalforth is coming with every intention of whispering passionate words of love to me?"

"I would shoot him through his black heart," Adam had answered with every appearance of seriousness. "And then return to my book room."

"It is a very good thing Mr. Dalforth's attention is quite universally directed toward Athena," Persephone had answered. Their exchange had shifted from a little tense to playful so quickly that Athena was at a loss to explain when the change had occurred.

"For both of you," Adam had confirmed.

"Both of us?"

"After putting a ball through Mr. Dalforth's chest, I would have found it necessary to lock you in the West Tower of Falstone Castle," Adam explained, eating his breakfast as though nothing untoward was being discussed.

"The one overlooking the gibbet?" Persephone had smiled as she'd asked the question to which she quite obviously knew the answer.

"To discourage any would-be suitors, my dear," Adam had answered. "You are, it seems, far too tempting for your own good if any man would even consider crossing me in his desperation to secure your affections."

"And it does not say much for this hypothetical gentleman's powers of observation," Persephone had added. "That my affections are not obtainable by anyone other than my husband should be obvious to even the thickest of individuals."

Adam gave Persephone a look that made Athena blush, though she was still at a loss to say precisely why. Persephone, Athena had noticed, was blushing as well. Adam had that effect on his wife.

Athena did not believe Mr. Dalforth had ever brought a blush to her cheeks. Harry had on more than one occasion—a look, the tone of his voice, that time he had held her hand in the theater. Athena felt her face heat at the reminder. Not only had she blushed but her heart had pounded and raced. It was the sort of reaction she ought to have been having to Mr. Dalforth if he was, indeed, to be her future husband.

A speeding pulse and a flushed countenance had always been part of her imagined courtship. When the butler announced Mr. Dalforth, Athena concentrated on her reaction, ready to analyze every minute change. Except there was no change. Athena had absolutely no discernible reaction to him. It was a depressing realization. She was conceivably on the verge of receiving an offer from a gentleman she was little better than indifferent to.

The tea was interminable. The excellent food provided by Adam's highly skilled chef tasted vaguely like air and water, tasteless and unnoticed. Athena tried to calm the almost frantic pulse pounding in her head. How had she come to be in such a situation? What was she going to do about it? She had difficulty imagining herself married to Mr. Dalforth, but what other prospects did she have?

"Might we take a turn about the garden?" Mr. Dalforth requested after the nerve-racking tea had been consumed.

Persephone gave her approval of the suggestion, though Athena thought she seemed reluctant. Why was that? Or had Athena imagined the hesitation?

She and Mr. Dalforth walked to the garden in what felt to Athena to be a very awkward silence. He seemed uneasy, nervous even. Could he be planning to propose?

Oh, please no, Athena silently thought, her panic increasing by the moment. She had not sorted out the situation, had not determined what to do. Could she accept Mr. Dalforth's offer knowing her heart was not involved? Could she refuse him knowing their engagement was talked of openly in society as an inevitable thing? Her reputation would suffer. And there was no guarantee she would ever receive another offer, as she was not at all certain Adam would allow her another Season.

"Miss Lancaster," Mr. Dalforth began.

Athena tried to take deeper breaths, though her lungs seemed determined to deprive her of air.

"I have grown fond of you these past weeks," he continued.

Fond. The word was monumentally disappointing. Athena, it seemed, was not the only one of them who was not in love. What a disaster!

"I realize that my attention could not possibly have gone unnoted, and I am aware that many in society have begun speculating as to my intentions and your expectations."

It was not very romantic as proposals went. Was nothing about this destined to match what she had always anticipated?

He paused as if expecting her to respond. "I do believe it is talked of," Athena managed.

"May I be candid with you?" Mr. Dalforth asked, suddenly quite urgent and glancing at her, his forehead creased.

"Of course," Athena answered. If she did not mistake his expression, Mr. Dalforth was very troubled by something. He certainly did not at all look like a besotted suitor.

They continued walking through the garden path, the chill air biting at Athena's face.

"When I first made your acquaintance at the beginning of the Little Season, I did so with the hope of coming to know you better. I liked what I had observed of you and wished to know if there was more I might like, might *more* than like. And I do like you."

"But not *more than like?*" Athena was beginning to suspect the direction of Mr. Dalforth's confession.

"I have no doubt raised expectations," he continued without answering her question. "If not specifically in your mind, then in society's at the least. And I do realize that, as a gentleman, I could not honorably fail to act on those expectations. Let me say this before I continue. I do believe that we are fond enough of one another and would deal well together."

That was very nearly *anti*romantic. She sensed a "but" coming and braced herself for it. No matter that she was not enamored of Mr. Dalforth, there was something very lowering about his not being enamored of her either.

"But I have always wished for . . . more in a wife. Not as a person," he quickly added. "I mean simply more in our feelings for one another. I had always imagined myself marrying for love."

He seemed to be making the admission apologetically. Athena remained silent, confused and upended. She wholeheartedly agreed with him, but what did that mean for their courtship or for his near-proposal?

"My parents' marriage was arranged, and though I think they have made a relatively successful union of it, I can see that there is something missing. They are like two individuals living parallel lives. I wish to marry my friend, someone with whom I share interests and ideas, someone with whom I can be a partner. One's entire countenance should light up, one's heart should react when his fiancée is nearby. There ought to be . . . something more."

"Mr. Dalforth," Athena said, trying to grab his attention. His eyes were focused ahead, his tone indicating he was not entirely aware he was speaking to anyone other than himself. "I completely agree with you. I have always wanted precisely that sort of marriage myself."

Reluctant relief swept Mr. Dalforth's features. "You realize that your reputation, even more than mine, would suffer if, after the speculation that has arisen, we do not make a match of it."

"I believe my heart would suffer even more if we did." Why Harry's face flashed through Athena's mind with that admission, she couldn't say. Perhaps because he of all people would understand, would empathize. Harry always seemed to understand how she was feeling. He had the uncanny ability to soothe her regardless of the circumstances. Harry would, undoubtedly, know how to relieve the sudden sadness in her heart.

She heard Mr. Dalforth sigh as if her answer had freed him from an onerous obligation. It was not a very flattering realization. Only the fact that she did not, particularly, wish to marry Mr. Dalforth kept her from feeling utterly depressed.

"I will be certain to show society that you and I remain friends, though I believe it would be best if we were seen to spend less time in one another's company," he said. "The Little Season will end very shortly, and by the time the Season is upon us, I believe expectations will have lessened significantly."

"I believe so," Athena acknowledged. There would be talk, she was certain of that. But an amicable split and the passage of time would help squelch any gossip that might arise.

Mr. Dalforth left a few minutes later after taking his leave of Persephone. Knowing she was bidding farewell to the only gentleman who would probably ever court her, Athena ought to have felt more disappointed. Mostly she felt tired, worn down from weeks of worry and uncertainty. She'd had her chance to find love, and it had slipped away.

She had the almost overwhelming urge to cry, though she could not say precisely why. And she wished almost desperately for Harry.

* * *

"You have a letter, Harry." Jane held the missive out to him with a look of mischievous curiosity on her face. "It is franked by the Duke of Kielder. Perhaps he is calling you out from several counties away."

"Not his style," Harry answered, reaching for the letter. "He prefers to see his victims tremble in terror. That cannot be accomplished through the post."

It was, indeed, franked by Adam, but, if Harry didn't miss his mark, the handwriting was feminine, though he knew it was not Athena's. Persephone, perhaps? That was odd. Harry hadn't ever received a letter from her.

He glanced up at Jane, watching him expectantly and hovering near the chair Harry occupied. "I believe I can read it without assistance," he hinted with a smile. "If I come across any difficult words I will consult the children's governess."

"You always were a bit too cheeky," Jane replied, smiling as broadly as ever. "Be warned. I shall use all my devious powers of persuasion to force a recounting out of you."

"I don't doubt it."

Jane made an overly dramatic face meant, he guessed, to represent those devious powers she had referenced, complete with wiggling fingers pointing supposedly threateningly in his direction, before turning and leaving him to the quiet of the sitting room.

Harry broke the seal on Persephone's letter and read quickly.

Harry,

Forgive me for intruding on your time with your sister, but I am writing most anxiously. The household is in utter chaos, I fear.

Artemis is unwell, an infectious fever not unlike the one Athena only recently recovered from. The state of Artemis's health has sent Adam's mother back into the country, she being most agitated when confronted with illness.

Daphne has grown oddly pensive, and not even Adam seems able to ascertain the reason for her very heavy state of mind.

Athena spends a great deal of time—far too much if you ask me—with tears hovering in her eyes. She has grown pale and does not smile as she once did. When I try to ask after her well-being, she simply tells me she is fine and changes the subject.

Adam is grown grumpy in this house full of emotional women, and I am at a loss. I know it is inexcusable of me, but I would ask a favor. Will you please return to London, even for only a week or so, until we are prepared to leave for Falstone Castle? If you could only keep Adam from being entirely irritable, then I could deal with the remaining crises.

Please come if you can.

Gratefully,
Persephone

Athena was apparently quite unhappy. Harry's heart wrenched at the thought. She had been like that after Persephone's wedding, the first time Harry had met her. But a few kind words of reassurance had set her mind at ease and lessened her burden. What could he possibly say or do to help her now? She despised him, distrusted him.

But then Persephone hadn't asked him to come for Athena's sake. He was to entertain and distract Adam, something that was remarkably easy to do. A few cheeky remarks about how nonthreatening he found his friend and a joke or two, and Adam would cheer up—as much as Adam ever did.

Harry could do that. But it would mean possibly seeing Athena again, seeing her with tears in her eyes, unhappy, and being unable to do anything to help.

Perhaps he was simply masochistic. Harry knew being back at Falstone House, being near her again, knowing she was angry with him, would be torturous. And yet he was already on his way to his room to pack.

Chapter 20

"I find myself struggling to believe that there is anything so enthralling about the back gardens as to have captured your undivided attention for a full thirty minutes."

Athena smiled a very little, turning slightly on the window seat to look at Persephone as she sat beside her. "I was lost in my thoughts, I suppose."

"A state you seem to regularly assume of late."

"I have had a great deal on my mind," Athena admitted, turning her gaze back to the frozen expanse of plants and walkways behind Falstone House, the window fogging with the warmth of her breath.

"This has been a busy few months for you," Persephone replied. "Some moments of reflection are expected. However, I would have thought those recollections would be . . . happier. You have seemed a bit unhappy, dearest. I have been reluctant to ask why, as I do not wish to pry, but I find I am growing concerned. It is very unlike you to be in the dismals for so long a period of time."

"I am not truly in the dismals—" Athena began the automatic protest. In all honesty, she was absolutely drowning in the dismals.

"Athena," Persephone interrupted, "I know you better than that."

Athena felt her sister take her hand, squeezing it the way she always had when they were young girls and Persephone was comforting her. There had been a great many circumstances during their childhood that had warranted reassurance: their mother's death, pending financial ruin, the defection of friends as their situation grew more destitute, loneliness. Persephone had been almost as much a mother during those times as she had been a sister. Athena needed a mother's wisdom and advice then more than ever.

Athena sighed, the sound heavy with resignation, even to her own ears. "These past weeks have not gone at all as I anticipated." The slightest catch in her voice gave away the level of her distress, and Persephone squeezed her fingers more firmly. It was comfort enough for Athena to continue. "I have dreamed for years about having a London Season, and instead of being delighted, I find I am . . . disappointed."

"Your experience did not match your dreams?" Persephone asked gently.

Athena shook her head, forcing back the sudden ache of tears in her eyes. Crying would not alleviate her frustration.

"What, precisely, has not occurred during these past weeks that you so desperately wish had?" Persephone asked.

"I didn't fall in love," Athena admitted before realizing she had spoken out loud. An embarrassed pink stained her cheeks— she could feel the heat of it.

In a voice even softer and kinder than she had used moments before, Persephone asked, "And how do you know you did not fall in love?"

Athena shifted to face Persephone again, confused at her question. "I would know if I was in love," she insisted.

"Oh, Athena," Persephone said, her tone suddenly very empathetic. "I have found that sometimes a person is the last to know when she is in love. One's heart does not always share its secrets with one's mind."

"But I know how I would feel if I were in love, and I don't feel that way," Athena protested. She had spent the past several days fluctuating between sadness and frustration. The pendulum was arcing once again.

Persephone's small laugh was ironic in timbre. "How would you know how it feels, Athena, if you have never been in love?"

That was an argument she had not considered. Did a person not know, instinctively, how love felt? She had always assumed so.

"Come," Persephone said, wrapping an arm around Athena's shoulder and all but forcing Athena to shift in her seat and lean against her. "It is time for an older-sister confession."

"Oh, dear," Athena answered, surprised that she was smiling, even if the effort was probably an abysmal failure.

"When I first met Adam—when I first *married* Adam, the two were essentially simultaneous, you know—I had what I felt was a pretty solid understanding of what love is and is not and what makes a happy and successful marriage. I had so many vivid and detailed dreams of my future."

Athena silently sighed. She had a great many dreams as well.

"I had always pictured living in a small, cozy home with a great many chickens just outside the front door and a large number of perpetually happy children running about the yard." Persephone gave Athena a look that clearly communicated that she understood the irony of those expectations. "My home ended up being a drafty castle that could easily house a substantial portion of the London populace. There are no chickens anywhere near the front doors of Falstone Castle and, thus far, no children.

"I had further envisioned myself married to a gentleman who was openly affectionate, inherently gentle, and constantly offering tender words of adoration."

Athena actually laughed out loud. Adam was the polar opposite of Persephone's described dream husband.

"Before you snort too loudly in derision, allow me a moment longer to further my embarrassment." But Persephone was laughing as well. She understood the discrepancy. "Father had always been that way with Mother, and it was, in my mind, firmly set as the only way two people in love interacted. I expected Adam to fit that mold so precisely that when he didn't, I was discouraged, disappointed.

"The more I got to know him, the more I found about him that I admired and liked and preferred in a husband over the traits I saw in our father. However, my predetermined ideas of how love plays out did not allow me to realize that I was falling in love with him. Adam is not openly affectionate, and, in public, he is neither gentle nor tender. He is, in his own way, all of those things. I simply needed to open my heart in order to see him as he really was."

"Then I should give up on all my dreams?" Athena couldn't prevent the break that accompanied her words.

"Oh, Athena." Persephone sounded a touch exasperated. "Artemis is supposed to be the dramatic one." She shook her head even as she pulled Athena closer. "You can have all those things that are most vital to you. Think of what it is you truly wish for in a companion, a friend, a lover—for a husband is all of those things. I believe you will find that the exact events surrounding falling in love can differ dramatically but have the same end result."

"I may not be swept off my feet by love is what you are saying." The words felt both disappointing and oddly hopeful. How was it possible to be both at the same time?

"Love may very well creep up on you," Persephone answered. "You will find yourself thinking about some gentleman who makes you smile just by smiling at you, who lightens your burdens simply with his presence, a gentleman whom you miss when you are apart and about whom you think during a separation, a gentleman you could not imagine never seeing again."

Persephone's words conjured up thoughts of Harry. She had missed him, thought of him in the days since he'd left. He had always brought a smile to her face, had always known how to make her feel better when she was discouraged or upset. But Persephone was supposedly talking about love. Harry was a friend.

Persephone continued. "And quite suddenly your stubborn mind will realize that while it was logically and systematically searching for love, your heart had already found it."

Her heart had already found love? But Persephone had described Harry. He was a friend, albeit a *good* friend, but nothing more. Wasn't he?

Athena closed her eyes, her mind immediately filled with thoughts of him. Harry had lightened her burden so many times. He had held her so comfortingly and gently the night of Mr. Rigby's assault. Harry had spent countless hours with her at Falstone Castle talking about more topics than she could even remember. He'd held her hand when she was in need of support. But where was the pounding heart, the symptoms of love and passion?

As if in response to her unspoken question, Athena's heart leaped in her chest. One single recollection brought about the phenomenon. Harry had held her hand at the theater that evening. He had caressed her fingers in a way that had made her heart stutter and lurch. Then it all flooded in, memories of a look or a word from him that had brought a stain to her cheeks or a greater rapidity to her pulse. She had always dismissed the effect before.

"Oh, my heavens," Athena whispered.

Persephone's arm tightened around Athena's shoulder. "I wondered when you would finally realize what I had long suspected."

"But he sabotaged me," Athena insisted, confusion warring with the heady rush of realization. "He intentionally introduced me only to gentlemen I could never have been happy with. How could I love someone who despises me enough to do that?"

"Athena," Persephone said, an almost scolding edge to her words. "I know Harry nearly as well as you do, and I do not for one moment believe him to be the sort of gentleman who would act as a saboteur."

"He as much as admitted it," Athena said.

"It is not Harry's actions that I doubt," Persephone answered. "It is his motivation. You believe he acted out of ill will or malice."

"You think differently?" Athena knew there was a hint of desperate hope in her voice, and she did not at all care. She had wanted to believe that Harry was still her friend ever since his departure from London, but realizing now how she had grown to love him, Athena needed to know that he did not despise her.

"I *know* differently," Persephone said. "Adam asked Harry to help with your come-out."

Being forced into service was almost as bad as purposefully undermining Athena's debut.

"Adam, unfortunately, is a little too unobservant to realize what he was asking of Harry," Persephone continued. "You know that Harry is as poor as a church mouse. His situation in many ways is even more desperate than ours was. A young lady without a dowry has a greater chance of marrying than a man who is destitute. He is labeled a fortune hunter by society, shunned by fathers of dowered young ladies, and too poor to marry a girl without a dowry. Harry has no title to induce a father to consider his suit and has no means of acquiring wealth of his own."

Athena nodded. She knew all that. Harry had been particularly empathetic when she had spoken of the difficulties they had passed through during the years of financial hardship. He had shared many of his own struggles and worries with her in return.

"Harry is a gentleman of the world, and though he can be quite absurd and jovial at times, he is realistic. He knows that, for all intents and purposes, he is considered ineligible."

Eligibility. It was one of the requirements on Athena's list; the list she had first concocted and shared with Harry. Would he have seen that as proof that his suit would not be welcomed?

"Looking back over the brief visit you made to Falstone Castle last Christmas and the time we all spent together last spring before the opening of the Season, I can see that Harry had grown very fond of you . . . perhaps more than fond. For Adam to ask Harry to help you find a husband when he himself would have liked to try for the position must have been torturous for Harry. I believe he did the best he could."

Athena wanted to believe it, but the arguments were too strong. "If he truly loved me, why did he not say so? Why did he not at least try?"

"He is practically penniless, Athena. A basic requirement for any suit to be considered acceptable is a gentleman's ability to support a wife."

"But I have a dowry," Athena said. "We would not be destitute."

"Men have pride, dear. Living off one's wife's wealth would sting tremendously."

"Is pride more important than love?" Athena asked, her hopefulness of a moment earlier dimmed by a feeling of sadness and frustration. Had Harry refused to court her because of pride?

Persephone sighed and gave Athena another squeeze. "You shall simply have to wait and see."

Chapter 21

THE FALSTONE BUTLER SMILED AS he opened the door for Harry. The house was, Harry noted, still standing. Nothing appeared to be broken or in disarray. For a household supposedly on the brink of utter chaos, the atmosphere was remarkably calm.

"Where might I find His Grumpiness?" Harry asked, enjoying the sight of Adam's very proper London butler attempting to keep a straight face.

"Their Graces are in the book room, Mr. Windover," was the very professional reply.

Harry nodded his acknowledgment and made his way up the stairs. A hauntingly familiar voice floating out of the drawing room stopped Harry in his tracks.

"Is Artemis finally sleeping?" Athena asked. Harry's heart thudded to hear her voice again. Heavens, how he'd missed her!

"Yes." He was pretty sure that was the governess.

Harry peeked discreetly around the corner of the doorway, hoping to see without being seen.

"Before she fell asleep, Miss Artemis asked me to give this to you." The governess held out a sheet of paper.

"A drawing?" Athena took the sheet and looked up at the governess.

Harry barely managed not to gasp. She was pale, just as Persephone's letter had indicated, and her eyes were weary, the spark he was so used to seeing there having dimmed. Harry desperately hoped the blame for that did not rest on his shoulders. Although, if Dalforth had broken her spirit, Harry was going to fillet the man!

"I believe it is meant to depict Miss Artemis in the throes of a painfully fatal disease," the governess explained.

Athena's mouth twitched ever so slightly, but she did not smile. "Artemis ever was the dramatic sister." Where was the laughter in her tone?

It took every ounce of Harry's self-control not to rush to her side and hold her to him, to coax a smile back to her face. He had to remind himself that he had not the right, nor would his attentions be welcomed. She was angry with him, after all.

Harry waited until Athena's eyes were directed at the drawing in her hand and moved quickly past the doorway and down the hallway until he reached the book room.

Adam looked not only surprised but happy when Harry walked in. Harry was grateful for that, though he knew Adam would not appreciate knowing as much.

"Perfect. Now I don't have to go to the Techneys' ball tonight."

"Yes, you do, Adam," Persephone replied with a smile. They were standing only a few feet apart, Adam with a book in his hand, Persephone looking out the window, though she turned her face to look at Adam as she spoke.

"But Harry is here," Adam pointed out, snapping his book shut.

"Harry is not Athena's guardian," Persephone said.

"She has a point, Adam," Harry said. He had come back to London in order to redirect Adam's grumpiness. There seemed little point in delaying the undertaking.

"Shut up, Harry."

Immediate success. Hearing Adam grumble wasn't nearly as satisfying as it had once been. Of late, *nothing* was quite as satisfying as it had once been. It was not the most promising vision of one's future.

"Remind me again why I volunteered to be responsible for your enormous family." Adam's mutterings were definitely directed toward Persephone. Harry, apparently, hadn't been as successful a diversion as he'd thought.

Persephone shrugged and turned back to look out the window. "Because you love your wife," she suggested, and Harry thought he caught a smile in her tone.

"Is that why?" Adam replied, setting his book down as he crossed to where she stood. He wrapped his arms around Persephone's waist. "And is that also the reason I am attending this infernal ball tonight?"

Only Adam could say the word *infernal* and still sound flirtatious. "Would you two like some privacy?" Harry asked.

"Yes," Adam declared at the same moment Persephone said, "Not yet."

"Apparently your marriage is not on the verge of collapse as I was led to believe," Harry said, eyeing the rather telling embrace to which he was witness.

Persephone spun in Adam's arms enough to look at Harry. "I only said Adam was grumpy." She looked decidedly guilty, and suddenly Harry was feeling very suspicious.

"You also wrote that Artemis was ill," Harry said.

"She has been ill, poor thing," Persephone confirmed, though a smile was growing on her face.

Adam rolled his eyes. "That 'poor thing' has begun enacting overly dramatic death scenes on her bed, so I think she is going to recover."

"And has Daphne returned from her state of abstraction?" Harry could hear the doubt in his voice. So much for coming to the rescue of a house in chaos.

"Actually, no," Adam grumbled. "The one source of logical conversation in this entire household, and she has turned moody."

"I am not sure if I am offended by that," Persephone said, looking up at Adam. "Are you not impressed by my conversation?"

"At the moment, I am not particularly interested in your *conversation*."

Harry shook his head, feeling decidedly de trop. "You two really ought to get your own place."

"Leave and we'll have our own place."

Harry made a theatrical bow and turned to go.

"Wait, Harry," Persephone called as Harry was certain she would.

"Don't stop him; he was actually leaving. Do you have any idea how often I have tried to get him to do that?"

"You can toss him out onto the street in a minute, Adam," Persephone reassured him. "I did ask him to come back for a reason."

"And it apparently was not to relieve me of my onerous duties as sponsor and guardian to a suddenly weepy young lady."

"Weepy?" Harry asked without really intending to. She had appeared sad, but Harry hadn't realized that Athena had been crying enough for Adam to have taken note of it.

"That is why I wanted you to come back," Persephone said. She motioned for Harry to sit in the chair nearest the fireplace. She took Adam's hand and led him to the sofa where they sat, hand in hand.

"You think Harry can get the girl to buck up a little?" Adam asked doubtfully. "I am entirely in favor of inflicting painful punishments on Harry, but forcing him to take on a watery female seems a little harsh. Even for me."

"I do not think you would have to force him," Persephone replied. She had a look in her eye that Harry recognized. It was the same searching look he had fled from when Athena was ill.

"Oh, yes," Adam answered sarcastically, "because Harry is such a pattern-card of Christian charity."

"No, because Harry is in love with her."

"What!?"

Harry actually flinched at Adam's booming voice. "Thanks, Persephone," he mumbled.

"How long has *this* been going on?" Adam demanded.

It was not at all how Harry had imagined spending a few days in London. Adam was never supposed to have learned about Harry's feelings for Athena. The last thing Harry wanted was a "no fortune hunters" lecture from Adam, especially when he was in his overprotective guardian mode. Harry shrugged but didn't offer a definitive answer.

"I believe"—Persephone began. Harry gave her a look of warning that was completely ignored—"he has been quite fond of her almost from their first meeting. Though, if I had to guess, I would say he fell quite decidedly in love with her this past spring, before we all came to Town."

"Harry Claudius Windover." Adam had never called him by his full given name. Harry actually stared, wide-eyed. What on earth did *that* tone mean? Adam spoke quietly—entirely *too* quietly in Harry's opinion—but with an edge to his voice. "Do you mean to tell me that I have just endured weeks of society when I could have been at home, and all this time *you* were in love with Athena?"

Harry cleared his throat and opened his mouth to speak, but ended by simply shrugging again.

"You worthless piece of maggoty mutton," Adam growled. "I could have been home weeks ago if you'd just fessed up and married the girl. Bloody h—"

"Adam," Persephone interrupted, effectively cutting off the curse they both knew was coming.

"The idiot forced me into an extra two months of this rancid London! I actually had to read an impertinent proposal-by-letter, attend balls—*balls,* Persephone—endure an entire house

filled with weeping, emotional women when that blackguard"—
Adam pointed at Harry—"was *in love* with her the entire time.
If I had known, I would simply have handed the girl over and
been done with the whole thing."

"You expressly forbade fortune hunters," Harry pointed out.
If he brought the objection up on his own, Adam was less likely
to explode when he remembered that difficulty himself.

"And?" Adam asked, crossing his arms across his chest.

"And if any gentleman in the kingdom needs to marry for
money, I do." Harry rose abruptly from his seat and crossed to
the fireplace, the warmth radiating from it penetrating his thick
boots. "I know better than to contradict a directive from the
Duke of Kielder."

"If I thought you wanted to marry Athena for money, I would
run you through in a heartbeat," Adam declared, the sound of his
footsteps indicating he had risen as well and crossed closer to where
Harry was standing. "No lady should have to live her life knowing
her husband married her because he needed her fortune."

"But I do need the money, Adam." Harry kicked at a log in
the fireplace, sending sparks spiraling up into the chimney flue.
"I have needed money since the day I was born."

"Then it is a very good thing you fell in love with a girl who
has plenty."

"Like I said"—Harry turned to look at Adam—"a fortune
hunter."

Adam gave an exasperated sigh. "What an idiot. Well, I can
see I wasted a great deal of money on your education," Adam
muttered as he moved back toward the sofa.

"What?" Harry stuttered out the word. "*You* wasted money
on my education? What is that supposed to mean? How are
your money and my education remotely connected?"

Adam rolled his eyes as he sat down next to Persephone, who
was watching their exchange rather pointedly. "Your family has

been destitute for fifty years, Harry. How did you think you went through Harrow and Oxford without resorting to being a charity student?"

"Some sort of family trust." Harry automatically gave the answer he'd assumed to be true for twenty years.

"Yes, I trusted that your family wouldn't tell you about it," Adam muttered.

"*You* paid for my schooling?" Harry was torn between a surge of gratitude and the sting of injured pride. "You were only eight years old, Adam."

"My mother paid for Harrow," Adam answered, shrugging casually, but there was a surprising amount of emotion in his eyes that he was obviously trying to disguise. "I think she was so shocked that I actually had a friend that she couldn't bear the idea of your not being at Harrow with me. When she heard that you were going to be pulled out for financial reasons, she arranged a sort of silent scholarship. I found out about it and took it over personally just before we left for Oxford."

"I am *not* a charity case, Adam," Harry protested.

"I rather felt like the charity case myself," Adam said quietly. "I had to pay to have a friend. And I wasn't ever entirely sure you didn't stick around for the protection or because you felt like you owed me something. That doesn't say much for the value of my friendship, does it?"

"It was never like that," Harry insisted.

"It still is not like that," Adam corrected. "On my side, either. You are like family, Harry. I take care of my family—the ones who aren't imbeciles, anyway."

Harry smiled. Adam even took care of the imbeciles, though he would never admit it.

"If you had fallen in love with a penniless girl, I would have found a way to see to it that you could marry, Harry," Adam said, looking uncomfortable as he admitted to the kinder side of himself that he generally kept locked out of sight. "If it meant making up some dead relative of yours, or the girl's, or something like that, I would have done it. Gads, man, I already did. Athena has a pathetically enormous dowry. Problem solved."

"No, not solved. What marriage could be successful when one partner brings all the money and the other nothing but poverty?"

Persephone's laugh caught Harry entirely off guard. What could she possibly find funny?

"It sounds as though our marriage is doomed, Adam." Persephone grinned. "If only I hadn't been so poverty-stricken and you so lopsidedly rich. I'm afraid there is absolutely no chance for us."

Harry felt himself begin to smile again. "Touché," he acknowledged.

"Well, where's Athena?" Adam asked. "Let's get these two engaged so we can pack up and return to Falstone Castle."

"It's not that simple, Adam," Harry said. "Athena doesn't return my feelings."

Persephone laughed again. It was more of a snort, really. "Good heavens, Harry. Why do you think she has been so emotional since you left?"

"Because she is angry with me?" Harry replied.

"Because she finally realized she is in love with you and is afraid you won't ever come back," Persephone said. Harry looked for a twinkle of mischief in her eyes that would turn her words into a joke. Persephone was entirely serious.

"Are you certain?" Harry asked, his heart suddenly pounding in his neck.

"She told me so herself."

Harry had to sit down.

"You see, Harry, Athena has always had a very detailed picture in her mind of how she would meet the man of her dreams," Persephone said. "She was so anticipating an exact reenactment of her expectations, had been praying for it, in fact, that for a while she mistook her feelings entirely. It was not until you left that she began to realize what she had lost."

"She figured out that the man of her dreams doesn't exist?" There was something about the wording in Persephone's explanation that left Harry oddly deflated.

Adam muttered something under his breath.

"She realized you *are* the man of her dreams," Persephone said. "You simply arrived differently than she'd expected."

"How had she expected?" Harry asked, curious.

Persephone's expression turned thoughtful again. She eyed Harry rather closely as a slow smile slid across her face. "Harry," Persephone said, "listen closely. You are going to make the Techneys' ball magical."

Chapter 22

ATHENA SAT ON A CHAIR near the wall at the last ball of the Little Season very much the way she had at the first ball more than two months earlier. Adam was just behind her. Persephone was at his side, in contrast to her determined socializing of that evening so many weeks before. Mr. Dalforth had danced with her but, as they had decided was best, had not paid her any more attention than that. Several of the remaining members of Athena's court had already left London for their country homes. Mr. Howard was still in London providing nearly constant proof that his knowledge of trees was unparalleled in its enormity.

Sitting out the majority of her dances was not as disheartening as it had been when Athena had first embarked on her debut in society. She found, in fact, that she rather preferred it. Her mind was too full of Harry to spare any thoughts for conversing with a dancing partner.

She wondered about Harry. Would he come to Falstone Castle for Christmas as he had the year before? Persephone had been unsure. Did Harry really love her as Persephone thought he did? And did he love her enough?

Athena held back a sigh, reminding herself that time would tell and she would simply have to wait and see, hoping that her heart could endure the uncertainty. The anger she had felt at learning of Harry's role in the ceaseless flow of imbeciles she'd met since arriving in London had dissipated rather suddenly. After Persephone had voiced her theory about Harry's feelings for Athena, that frustration had seemed to vanish. Something in her had never truly believed that Harry had acted out of malice; to think that he might have acted out of love was a thought that gave her more hope than she could have imagined. If only he would return so she might know for sure.

She allowed her gaze to sweep the room. How easily she could have been seeing the ball she'd imagined so many times. The room was every bit as lovely, the dresses as colorful, the music as enchanting as her dreams had painted them. But *he* was missing.

The dancers spun and crossed in the intricate patterns of a dance as Athena watched. Through a break in the line of dancers, she thought she saw a face. A very familiar face. Athena's heart thumped painfully in her chest, but the dancers shifted and closed the gap again, and she could not be sure.

Athena moved slightly in her chair, searching. Surely she would have known if Harry had returned to London. She must have been mistaken. And yet the gentleman she'd seen looked so very much like him.

She attempted to appear nonchalant as she frantically studied each face across the room every time the dancers afforded her a glimpse.

There again! She was nearly certain it was him after all. Athena pressed a hand to her throat where her heart was pounding a frantic rhythm. Harry had come back! Would he come and speak to her? Did he wish to even see her? Had she realized her own heart too late?

The orchestra played out the last bars of the current dance, and the participants applauded appropriately. Only a moment and the next set would begin. With whom would Harry dance?

Would he dance at all? Would she be able to steal a glimpse of him once more?

Athena wasn't even sure where he'd gone, she'd lost sight of him.

"Miss Lancaster."

Athena looked quickly in Mr. Howard's direction as his voice interrupted her search.

"Mr. Howard," she replied politely, if a little rushed.

Mr. Howard began talking, probably about trees. Athena's eyes had returned to the crowd. In an instant she saw him. He was still across the room but drawing closer. Their eyes met, and Athena could feel her heart pounding harder in her chest. She couldn't pull her eyes from him, and he didn't look away.

As she watched Harry draw nearer, their eyes locked. He didn't smile, but he didn't look upset, either. What was he thinking? Was he happy to see her?

Please let him be happy about it, she silently pleaded.

"Miss Lancaster?" Mr. Howard's voice broke into her thoughts.

She spared him only the briefest of glances, just long enough to register that he was watching her in obvious expectation, though she wasn't sure of what. Her eyes had already returned to Harry, now only a few steps away.

Harry's eyes hadn't left her. Athena was very nearly certain her heart had sped to twice its normal pulse. Every inch of her seemed to have begun trembling.

A smile spread across Harry's face, and Athena felt the telling blush that spread across her cheeks and down her neck. Harry's smile! She smiled in return but felt unaccountably nervous, almost as if she'd suddenly become very shy in his presence.

"Miss Lancaster?" Mr. Howard's attempts to gain her attention had grown more urgent.

But Harry was at her side, and Athena could not look away. *Please love me,* she silently begged. What would she do if she had lost him already?

"Mr. Howard," Harry said to Athena's eager, if ignored, conversational partner.

"Mr. Windover."

"Forgive me for being rude, but I do believe this dance has been promised to me," Harry said.

Athena wasn't sure if Mr. Howard replied, the pounding of her heart having deafened her. Harry held his hand out to her and smiled. Athena placed her hand in his, an amazing sensation of tingling and awareness spreading up her arm in waves and pulses.

The phenomenon continued throughout the dance. Every time the steps required their hands to touch, she tingled at the contact. Neither of them spoke a word. Their eyes met at every opportunity, and his smile, different from the laughing smiles he so often produced, always greeted her when the movements of the dance brought them back together. That smile made her blush all over again.

It was her dream come to life: a meeting of eyes across a ballroom, a pounding heart, an undeniable awareness. All that time it was Harry! How had she missed it?

Her heart and mind in a jumble of emotions, Athena was returned to her seat as the dance ended. Persephone and Adam were in the midst of a conversation and did not acknowledge Harry and Athena's return.

Harry bowed quite formally, smiled, and walked away.

Athena watched him go, confused. He had not actually spoken to her, not so much as a word. She longed to call him back but was afraid that her plea would be met with rejection. Had he danced with her out of obligation? No. She could not believe that. Then why, she asked herself, had he left?

"Are you all right, Athena?" Persephone asked. "You look a little pale."

"I think I will just take a moment in the withdrawing room," Athena said, rising a little shakily.

"Would you like me to come with you?" Persephone offered.

"No," Athena insisted. "I'll be fine."

She moved swiftly but as inconspicuously as possible from the ballroom. She did not wish to draw attention but very much feared if she did not escape quickly, the tears would fall before she was away. She knew that crying at a ball was not permitted.

* * *

HARRY SAW ATHENA SLIP OUT of the ballroom. He moved quickly. Intercepting her without being seen was going to be difficult, but he absolutely had to. There was too much that needed to be said. And he needed to hold her, if she would let him. He needed the comfort of her in his arms. That need had nearly undone him as they'd danced. It was not at all the done thing to embrace one's partner in the middle of a ballroom in the midst of a dance. But he had been very sorely tempted.

Athena was moving quickly, but Harry had the advantage of familiarity; he had attended many balls and musicales at the Techneys' home. The hallway was deserted—a happy circumstance, as he had no desire to attempt to circumvent a crowd.

Harry reached her from behind just as she passed the doorway to a small sewing room, one not being used as part of the ball. Harry quickly took hold of her hand and pulled her inside. He felt Athena stiffen and immediately begin pulling away.

"Athena," he whispered, pulling her close enough for her to hear him.

"Harry," she answered, turning to look at him, eyes wide, voice full of surprise. "I—"

He laid a finger on her lips, stopping her words as he closed the door to the room. It was a potentially compromising situation, but there were some things he needed to say to her, and an audience would be most unwelcome.

Talking was what he ought to have been doing, but touching her lips was proving very distracting. Harry's eyes traced every inch of her beloved face—her brilliant green eyes, the tiny bewitching mouth, the dimple he knew would appear if only she would smile.

"You came back," Athena said, Harry's hand having traveled away from her lips to stroke a perfect gold ringlet framing her face.

He was having a very difficult time breathing. He was touching her. Touching Athena. And not in a very brotherly way. He had never once held Jane's hair between his fingers or brushed his hand along her cheek.

"I was so afraid you wouldn't," Athena continued. "And then I saw you, and I was afraid you wouldn't come talk to me. And you didn't. Talk, that is. And I thought—"

"Athena," Harry said again, still a whisper, his eyes memorizing her features.

"Harry?" Her voice broke a little, her tone uncertain.

"Athena." His heart was pounding so loudly he was sure she could hear it. He was holding her face in his hands, as he'd dreamed of doing so many times.

Harry closed his eyes, forcing several long, deep breaths. Stepping away from her would have been best, but he couldn't bring himself to do it.

"Harry, are you angry with me?"

"Angry with you?" His shock pulled Harry's eyes open.

"You wouldn't even talk to me," she said, moisture pooling in her eyes. "In the ballroom. You just left. I know I was curt with you the last time I saw you, but—"

"Oh, Athena." He shook his head, a smile inching its way across his face. "You had every right to be curt with me—angry, even. I should have been more honest with you. You had a right to know why I introduced you to the gentlemen I did."

Athena looked away from him, a tear slipping from her eyes as she did. Harry knew in an instant she'd imagined some horrid motivation behind what he'd done.

"Athena, darling," he whispered, pulling her into his arms, hoping to give as much comfort as he knew he would receive from the embrace. Harry wasn't entirely sure his heart could speed up any more than it did in that moment without bringing on his rather premature demise. "I am sorry. I shouldn't have been so duplicitous, but I simply couldn't bear the idea of finding you a husband."

"Why not?" she asked, her head resting against his chest.

It was confession time. If Persephone had been mistaken and Athena was not, in fact, in love with him, Harry's next words might very well signal the end of all his hopes. He could not, however, deny the fact that she had not uttered a single objection as he'd touched her hair, caressed her face, or held her to him.

"Because I wanted you myself," Harry admitted on a whisper. "I have loved you almost from the first time I met you, Athena. And if I did not have a chance to win you, I at least wanted you to recognize the sort of gentlemen who could never make you happy."

"You wanted me to be happy?" she looked up at him, and Harry was certain he saw hope in her eyes.

"That is all I have ever wanted."

"Then why did you not court me yourself?"

"Adam expressly forbade any fortune hunters from soliciting your hand," Harry answered.

Athena cut him off before he could continue. "But you are not a fortune hunter. Mr. Rigby was a fortune hunter. You could never be so cruel and unfeeling and inherently dishonest."

Harry felt his smile spread wider. "Adam told me essentially the same thing." Harry locked his hands together behind

Athena, relishing the warmth of her so close to him. "Although he used words I would not dare repeat in front of a lady."

"Then Adam approves?" She smiled, though the dimple was not yet evident.

"I think Adam would condone and assist a kidnapping and elopement if he thought I would go along with the idea."

The slightest hint of a blush suddenly appeared on Athena's face, her expression instantly almost bashful. Harry was beyond intrigued. "I wouldn't object to a kidnapping," she said quietly. She smiled as she spoke, and that one enchanting dimple made its long-awaited appearance.

"I have wanted to do this for ages," Harry whispered, more to himself than to Athena.

"Do what?" she asked, the last word cutting off mid-syllable as Harry took hold of her face and leaned closer to her.

Heart racing and pounding again, he bent toward her and slowly, gently kissed the dimple just at the corner of her mouth. He heard and felt her sigh and knew it was a lost cause. He had intended only to talk with her. He'd get back to the talking eventually.

The slightest shift was all that was necessary for his lips to touch hers. He wanted to run his fingers through her hair, but that tiny part of his mind that was still functioning rationally knew that such obvious damage to her appearance would not easily be put to rights. He would not subject her to the gossip that would create. Harry contented himself with touching her face, her neck, wrapping his arms around her and simply holding her to him.

Athena's arms hooked around his neck as she returned his kisses with obvious enthusiasm. Being romantically courted may have been Athena's dream, but being kissed like that by Athena had long been Harry's.

He smiled as he pulled away. Harry kept his hands on her shoulders, his arms a little stiff, in order to maintain the necessary distance. Closed doors and heartfelt confession were, it seemed, a dangerous combination. He would need to take extra precautions to avoid such things until everything was official and such liberties were permitted.

"Oh, Harry," Athena said, her voice a little breathless, her face flushed still.

Harry smiled, happiness permeating every inch of him. She moved toward him, and he stiffened his arms, preventing her from approaching. "You need to stay over there." He laughed lightly. "Your lips are temptation enough without the smell of violets undermining my self-control."

"Then you won't be kidnapping me after all?" Athena asked, her eyes twinkling and alive again. The weight he'd seen there only that afternoon as he'd observed her in the drawing room had vanished, and Harry's heart sang with relief.

"No. But I would very much like to marry you," he said. "I have loved you without hope for so long. And now . . . Adam and Persephone approve. All I need to know is if you love me—if you love me enough to marry a man who has absolutely nothing to offer you."

"You have yourself to offer, Harry," Athena corrected. "That is what I want."

"Will you marry me, my love?"

Athena smiled as brightly as Harry ever remembered seeing and nodded.

In an instant she was in his arms, holding tightly to him and laughing joyously. It was music.

"Are you two almost done in there?" Adam's voice penetrated the cocoon of privacy Harry had felt surrounding them in the same instant the door opened. "You could have gotten married and raised half your family in the amount of time you've taken."

Harry kept Athena in his arms as he chuckled and faced his friend. "We've only been in here ten minutes, Adam."

"Long enough for me to insist you marry her," Adam pointed out. "I'll get you a special license. You can be married tonight. We'll wrap this up, and we can all go home."

"No, Adam," Harry said. "Post the banns, we'll marry at Falstone Chapel. At Christmas."

"Christmas!" Adam stepped closer to them, his stance defiant. "That is a full month away, you sniveling worm."

"It will be a very busy month, I assure you." Harry tightened his hold on Athena, even kissing the top of her head.

Adam's expression shifted into the seething, bubbling calm that always indicated he was moments from slicing some unsuspecting person's throat. "*Busy* in what way?" he asked, his eyes pointedly moving to Harry's arms wrapped very snuggly around Athena.

"Nothing untoward, I assure you. I simply think Athena ought to be courted like any young lady would wish to be." Adam raised an eyebrow. "Under the watchful eye of her guardian, of course," Harry added.

"You mean I have to watch this sentimental muck?" Adam looked absolutely repulsed. "For an entire month!"

"I am certain Persephone would take turns with you." Harry could feel Athena laughing as he spoke.

"I will not have Falstone Castle turned into a monument to romantic nonsense," Adam declared, spinning back toward the door. "Persephone!"

She slipped in from around the corner, grinning in obvious amusement. "Yes?"

"He wants a month." Adam pointed at Harry. "A month of *that.*"

"They are courting, dear," Persephone laughed. "*That* is to be expected."

"Yes, well, being thrown in the dungeon or hanged in the gibbet is also to be expected," Adam threatened. "Worthless heap of rubbish," he ended on a mutter.

"I am certain you can find ample distractions, Adam," Persephone said.

"I should have thrown him out decades ago."

"Yes, you probably should have," Persephone replied. "But now you are stuck with him. It is best you endure until he takes his bride home."

"And I will not wait around until that pile of rotting timbers on his estate is livable, you hear me?" Adam gave Harry a very pointed look. "Pick any Kielder holding—except the Castle—and take yourselves off as soon as the register is signed. Live there as long as it takes. I will not endure the sight of newlyweds."

It was an offer of a place to live until Harry's estate was put to rights. Harry recognized that, as well as the need Adam felt to justify the generosity by cloaking it in a mask of irritation. Life had not been kind to Adam, but Harry was realizing that he, himself, was fortunate indeed. He would never have thought while he was being pummeled by a gang of bullies his first year at Harrow that the beating would prove to be one of the best things that had ever happened to him. Adam had come to the rescue then, and the friendship that followed had changed Harry's life for the better.

"In the interest of our continued existence, I'll do just that," Harry assured Adam, smiling his gratitude, knowing Adam would not appreciate having it spoken out loud.

Adam nodded, precisely the way he always did when acknowledging what Harry had left unspoken.

"I believe if we put our minds to it, we could leave for Falstone Castle in the morning," Persephone said. "If we pack the essentials and have the staff send up the rest afterward, we could manage it."

"Perfect," Adam declared. "First light, Harry."

Harry nodded. Adam had always taken him to Falstone to save Harry the cost of taking a public conveyance. The trip would be even more appreciated than before with Athena there for company.

"And you can get on with the business of courting your future wife." Persephone smiled.

"Gladly," Harry answered.

Persephone and Adam stepped from the room first. Harry lifted Athena's hand to his lips. With the door open, kissing her as he truly wished to was no longer an option.

"Oh, Harry," Athena said. "All those years I prayed that I would find a wonderful, loving gentleman. I watched and waited and worried. And all along, the answer was you."

Harry smiled at her. He rather enjoyed being the answer to a prayer. "Sometimes, I think heaven has to hit us over the head to get our attention. Adam regularly takes on that duty himself."

"I love you, Harry," Athena said, touching his face with the hand he was not holding.

"And I love you," he answered, squeezing her fingers before pulling her arm through his and walking quite properly with her on his arm.

"Are you really going to court me?" Athena asked, smiling at him.

"Quite extensively," Harry confirmed. "I only hope I meet the requirements on that rather long list of yours."

"You should," she answered. "You're the one who wrote it for me, after all."

"So I did," Harry chuckled. "And I believe we ought to work on a few more specific items for that list."

Athena's cheeks pinked once more, something Harry thoroughly enjoyed seeing. "Will I like these specifics?"

"You will love these specifics."

Athena leaned against his arm. "I think we are going to be very happy, Harry."

"Yes. And we are going to make Adam absolutely miserable for the next few weeks."

"I think that sounds delightful."

Harry stopped in the midst of the hallway, checking quickly to see that they were alone. Courting, after all, invariably involved a few stolen kisses. "It will be entirely delightful," he said and kissed her quite thoroughly.

Life, at times, could be very nearly perfect.

About the Author

Photo by Claire Waite.

Sarah M. Eden read her first Jane Austen novel in elementary school and has been an Austen Addict ever since. Fascinated by the Regency era in English history, Eden became a regular in the Regency section of the reference department at her local library, painstakingly researching this extraordinary chapter in history. Eden is an award-winning author of short stories and was a Whitney Award Finalist for her novel *Seeking Persephone* (2008). You can visit her at www.sarahmeden.com.